Afternoon
in the Jungle

Afternoon in the Jungle

THE SELECTED SHORT STORIES OF

Albert Maltz

Liveright　　New York

———————————

FOR MY WIFE, ESTHER

———————————

1. 987654321

Standard Book Number: 87140-525-3

Library of Congress Catalog Card Number: 74131272

Designed by Barbara K. Grenquist

Manufactured in the United States of America

Contents

Man
on a Road

Man
on a Road

At about four in the afternoon I crossed the bridge at Gauley, West Virginia, and turned the sharp curve leading into the tunnel under the railroad bridge. I had been over this road once before and knew what to expect — by the time I entered the tunnel I had my car down to about ten miles an hour. But even at that speed I came closer to running a man down than I ever have before. This is how it happened.

The patched, macadam road had been soaked

"Man on a Road" was first published in 1935.

through by an all-day rain and now it was as slick as
ice. In addition, it was quite dark — a black sky and
a steady, swishing rain made driving impossible without headlights. As I entered the tunnel a big cream-
colored truck swung fast around the curve on the other
side. The curve was so sharp that his headlights had
given me no warning. The tunnel was short and nar-
row, just about passing space for two cars, and before
I knew it he was in front of me with his big, front
wheels over on my side of the road.

I jammed on my brakes. Even at ten miles an hour
my car skidded, first toward the truck and then, as I
wrenched on the wheel, in toward the wall. There it
stalled. The truck swung around hard, scraped my
fender, and passed through the tunnel about an inch
away from me. I could see the tense face of the young
driver with the tight bulge of tobacco in his cheek
and his eyes glued on the road. I remember saying to
myself that I hoped he'd swallow that tobacco and go
choke himself.

I started my car and shifted into first. It was then
I saw for the first time that a man was standing in front
of my car about a foot away from the inside wheel. It
was a shock to see him there. "For Chrissakes," I said.

My first thought was that he had walked into the
tunnel after my car had stalled. I was certain he hadn't
been in there before. Then I noticed that he was standing profile to me with his hand held up in the hitch-
hiker's gesture. If he had walked into that tunnel, he'd
be facing me — he wouldn't be standing sideways
looking at the opposite wall. Obviously I had just

missed knocking him down and obviously he didn't know it. He didn't even know I was there.

It made me run weak inside. I had a picture of a man lying crushed under a wheel with me standing over him knowing it was my car.

I called out to him "Hey!" He didn't answer me. I called louder. He didn't even turn his head. He stood there, fixed, his hand up in the air, his thumb jutting out. It scared me. It was like a story by Bierce where the ghost of a man pops out of the air to take up his lonely post on a dark country road.

My horn is a good, loud, raucous one and I knew that the tunnel would re-double the sound. I slapped my hand down on that little black button and pressed as hard as I could. The man was either going to jump or else prove that he was a ghost.

Well, he wasn't a ghost — but he didn't jump either. And it wasn't because he was deaf. He heard that horn all right.

He was like a man in a deep sleep. The horn seemed to awaken him only by degrees, as though his whole consciousness had been sunk in some deep recess within himself. He turned his head slowly and looked at me. He was a big man, about thirty-five with a heavy-featured face — an ordinary face with a big, fleshy nose and a large mouth. The face didn't say much. I wouldn't have called it kind or brutal or intelligent or stupid. It was just the face of a big man, wet with rain, looking at me with eyes that seemed to have a glaze over them. Except for the eyes you see faces like that going into the pit at six in the morning, or coming out of a steel mill or foundry where heavy work is done. I couldn't understand that glazed quality in his eyes. It wasn't the glassy stare of a drunken man, or the wild, mad glare I saw once in the eyes of a woman in a fit of violence. I could only think of a man I once knew who had died of cancer. Over his eyes, in the last days, there was the same dull glaze, a far away, absent look as though behind the blank, outward film there was a secret flow of past events on which his mind was focused. It was this same look that I saw in the man on the road.

When at last he heard my horn, the man stepped very deliberately around the front of my car and came toward the inside door. The least I expected was that he would show surprise at an auto so dangerously close to him. But there was no emotion to him whatsoever. He walked slowly, deliberately, as though he had been expecting me and then bent his head down to see under the top of my car. "Kin yuh give me a lift, friend?" he asked me.

I saw his big, horse teeth chipped at the ends and stained brown by tobacco. His voice was high-pitched and nasal with the slurred, lilting drawl of the deep South. In West Virginia few of the town folk seem to speak that way. I judged he had been raised in the mountains.

I looked at his clothes — an old cap, a new blue work shirt, and dark trousers, all soaked through with rain. They didn't tell me much.

I must have been occupied with my thoughts about him for some time, because he asked me again.

"Ahm goin' to Weston," he said. "Are you a'goin' thataway?"

As he said this, I looked into his eyes. The glaze had disappeared and now they were just ordinary eyes, brown and moist.

I didn't know what to reply. I didn't really want to take him in — the episode had unnerved me and I wanted to get away from the tunnel and from him too. But I saw him looking at me with a patient, almost humble glance. The rain was streaked on his face and he stood there asking for a ride and waiting in simple concentration for my answer. I was ashamed to tell him "no." Besides, I was curious. "Climb in," I said.

He sat down beside me, placing a brown paper package on his lap. We started out of the tunnel.

From Gauley to Weston is about a hundred miles of as difficult mountain driving as I know — a five mile climb to the top of a hill, then five miles down, and then up another. The road twists like a snake on the run and for a good deal of it there is a jagged cliff on one side and a drop of a thousand feet or more on the other. The rain, and the small rocks crumbling from the mountain sides and littering up the road, made it very slow going. But in the four hours or so that it took for the trip I don't think my companion spoke to me half-a-dozen times.

I tried often to get him to talk. It was not that he wouldn't talk, it was rather that he didn't seem to hear me — as though as soon as he had spoken, he would slip down into that deep, secret recess within himself. He sat like a man dulled by morphine. My conversation, the rattle of the old car, the steady pour of rain were all a distant buzz — the meaningless, outside world that could not quite pierce the shell in which he seemed to be living.

As soon as we had started, I asked him how long he had been in the tunnel.

"Ah don' know," he replied. "A good tahm, ah reckon."

"What were you standing there for — to keep out of the rain?"

He didn't answer. I asked him again, speaking very loudly. He turned his head to me. "Excuse me, friend," he said, "did you say somethin'?"

"Yes," I answered. "Do you know I almost ran you over back in that tunnel?"

"No-o," he said. He spoke the word in that breathy way that is typical of mountain speech.

"Didn't you hear me yell to you?"

"No-o." He paused. "Ah reckon ah was thinkin'."

"Ah reckon you were," I thought to myself. "What's the matter, are you hard of hearing?" I asked him.

"No-o," he said, and turned his head away looking out front at the road.

I kept right after him. I didn't want him to go off again. I wanted somehow to get him to talk.

"Looking for work?"

"Yessuh."

He seemed to speak with an effort. It was not a difficulty of speech, it was something behind, in his mind, in his will to speak. It was as though he couldn't keep touch between his world and mine. Yet when he did answer me, he spoke directly and coherently. I didn't know what to make of it. When he first came into the car I had been a little frightened. Now I only felt terribly curious and a little sorry.

"Do you have a trade?" I was glad to come to that question. You know a good deal about a man when you know what line of work he follows, and it always leads to further conversation.

"Ah ginerally follows the mines," he said.

"Now," I thought, "we're getting somewhere."

But just then we hit a stretch of unpaved road where the mud was thick and the ruts were hard to follow. I had to stop talking and watch what I was doing. And when we came to paved road again, I had lost him.

I tried again to make him talk. It was no use. He didn't even hear me. Then, finally, his silence shamed me. He was a man lost somewhere within his own soul, only asking to be left alone. I felt wrong to keep thrusting at his privacy.

So for about four hours we drove in silence. For me those hours were almost unendurable. I have never seen such rigidity in a human being. He sat straight up in the car, his outward eye fixed on the road in front, his inward eye seeing nothing. He didn't know I was in the car, he didn't know he was in the car at all, he didn't feel the rain that kept sloshing in on him through the rent in the side curtains. He sat like a slab of molded rock and only from his breathing could I be sure that he was alive. His breathing was heavy.

Only once in that long trip did he change his posture. That was when he was seized with a fit of coughing. It was a fierce, hacking cough that shook his big body from side to side and doubled him over like a child with the whooping cough. He was trying to cough something up — I could hear the phlegm in his chest — but he couldn't succeed. Inside him there was an ugly scraping sound as though cold metal were being rubbed on the bone of his ribs, and he kept spitting and shaking his head.

It took almost three minutes for the fit to subside. Then he turned around to me and said, "Excuse me, friend." That was all. He was quiet again.

I felt awful. There were times when I wanted to stop the car and tell him to get out. I made up a dozen good excuses for cutting the trip short. But I couldn't do it. I was consumed by a curiosity to know what was wrong with the man. I hoped that before we parted, perhaps even as he got out of the car, he would tell me what it was or say something that would give me a clue.

I thought of the cough and wondered if it were T.B. I thought of cases of sleeping sickness I had seen and of a boxer who was punch-drunk. But none of these things seemed to fit. Nothing physical seemed to explain this dark, terrible silence, this intense, all-exclusive absorption within himself.

Hour after hour of rain and darkness!

Once we passed the slate dump of a mine. The rain had made the surface burst into flame and the blue and red patches flickering in a kind of witch glow on a hill of black seemed to attract my companion. He turned his head to look at it, but he didn't speak, and I said nothing.

And again the silence and rain! Occasionally a mine tipple with the cold, drear, smoke smell of the dump and the oil lamps in the broken-down shacks where the miners live. Then the black road again and the shapeless bulk of the mountains.

We reached Weston at about eight o'clock. I was tired and chilled and hungry. I stopped in front of a café and turned to the man.

"Ah reckon this is hit," he said.

"Yes," I answered. I was surprised. I had not expected him to know that we had arrived. Then I tried a final plunge. "Will you have a cup of coffee with me?"

"Yes," he replied, "thank you, friend."

The "thank you" told me a lot. I knew from the way he said it that he wanted the coffee but couldn't pay for it; that he had taken my offer to be one of hospitality and was grateful. I was happy I had asked him.

We went inside. For the first time since I had come upon him in the tunnel he seemed human. He didn't talk, but he didn't slip inside himself either. He just sat down at the counter and waited for his coffee. When it came, he drank it slowly, holding the cup in both hands as though to warm them.

When he had finished, I asked him if he wouldn't like a sandwich. He turned around to me and smiled. It was a very gentle, a very patient smile. His big, lumpy face seemed to light up with it and become understanding and sweet and gentle.

The smile shook me all through. It didn't warm me — it made me feel sick inside. It was like watching a corpse begin to stir. I wanted to cry out, "My God, you poor man!"

Then he spoke to me. His face retained that smile and I could see the big, horse teeth stained by tobacco.

"You've bin right nice to me, friend, an' ah do appreciate it."

"That's all right," I mumbled.

He kept looking at me. I knew he was going to say something else and I was afraid of it.

"Would yuh do me a faveh?"

"Yes," I said.

He spoke softly. "Ah've got a letter here that ah done writ to mah woman, but ah can't write very good. Would you all be kind enough to write it ovah for me so it'd be proper like?"

"Yes," I said, "I'd be glad to."

"A kin tell you all know how to write real well," he said, and smiled.

"Yes."

He opened his blue shirt. Under his thick woolen underwear there was a paper fastened by a safety pin. He handed it to me. It was moist and warm and the damp odor of wet cloth and the slightly sour odor of his flesh clung to it.

I asked the counterman for a sheet of paper. He brought me one. This is the letter I copied. I put it down here in his own script.

My dere wife —

    i am awritin this yere leta to tell you somethin i did not tell you afore i lef frum home. There is a cause to wy i am not able to get me any job at the mines. i told you hit was frum work abein slack. But this haint so.

    Hit comes frum the time the mine was shut down an i worked in the tunel nere Gauley Bridge where the company is turnin the river inside the mounten. The mine supers say they wont hire any men war worked in thet tunel.

    Hit all comes frum thet rock thet we all had to dril. Thet rock was silica and hit was most all of hit glass. The powder frum this glass has got into the lungs of all the men war worked in thet tunel thru their breathin. And this has given to all of us a sickness. The doctors writ it down for me. Hit is silicosis. Hit makes the lungs to git all scab like and then it stops the breathin.

    Bein as our hom is a good peece frum town you ain't heerd about Tom Prescott and Hansy McCulloh having died two days back. But wen i heerd this i went to see the doctor.

    The doctor says i hev got me thet sickness like Tom Prescott and thet is the reeson wy i am coughin sometime. My lungs is agittin scab like. There is in all ova a hondred men war have this death sickness frum the tunel. It is a turible plague becus the doctor says this wud not be so if the company had gave us masks to ware an put a right fan sistem in the tunel.

So i am agoin away becus the doctor says i will be dead in about fore months.

i figger on gettin some work maybe in other parts. i will send you all my money till i caint work no mohr.

i did not want i should be a burdin upon you all at hum. So thet is wy i hev gone away.

i think wen you doan here frum me no mohr you orter go to your grandmaws up in the mountens at Kilney Run. You kin live there and she will take keer of you an the young one.

i hope you will be well an keep the young one out of the mines. Doan let him work there.

Doan think hard on me for agoin away and doan feel bad. But wen the young one is agrowed up you tell him wat the company has done to me.

i reckon after a bit you shud try to git you anotha man. You are a young woman yit.

Your loving husband,
Jack Pitckett.

When I handed him the copy of his letter, he read it over. It took him a long time. Finally he folded it up and pinned it to his undershirt. His big, lumpy face was sweet and gentle. "Thank you, friend," he said. Then, very softly, with his head hanging a little — "Ahm feelin' bad about this a-happenin' t'me. Mah wife was a good woman." He paused. And then, as though talking to himself, so low I could hardly hear it, "Ah'm feelin' right bad."

As he said this, I looked into his face. Slowly

the life was going out of his eyes. It seemed to recede and go deep into the sockets like the flame of a candle going into the night. Over the eyeballs came that dull glaze. I had lost him. He sat deep within himself in his sorrowful, dark absorption.

That was all. We sat together. In me there was only mute emotion — pity and love for him, and a cold, deep hatred for what had killed him.

Presently he arose. He did not speak. Nor did I. I saw his thick, broad back in the blue work shirt as he stood by the door. Then he moved out into the darkness and rain.

The Way
Things Are

The Way Things Are

I

The midsummer Louisiana sun was a red blotch in the hazy sky. To the three men in the open touring car it felt like a blowtorch suspended a foot above them. Two of the men lay sprawled out on the back seat with their coats off, with soggy handkerchiefs wrapped about their necks, and with their mouths sagging open as

---

"The Way Things Are" was first published in 1938.

though they were a pair of strangled fish. The third
man sat hunched over the wheel with a bandanna
around his forehead to keep the salt sweat out of his
eyes. The three men were a sheriff and his two deputies.
They were out to bring back a prisoner — at least,
that was what they supposed. They had really taken
the twenty-six mile drive over the sandy road because
Avery Smallwood had put in a telephone call. He had
said "Please bring two deputies, Mr. Tuckahue," and
Mr. Tuckahue had brought the two deputies. Beyond
that they didn't know why they had come.

Now, as they passed beyond the broad, flat fields
knee high with cotton plants as far back as the eye
could see, and passed beyond the last cluster of tumbledown shacks where the black sharecroppers lived, they
came abruptly to the magnificent grounds which surrounded the Smallwood home.

After the long drive over the sunbaked sand, the
house and the green grass and the tall shade trees that
lined the road — cypress and sycamore trees and huge
weeping willows with foliage like thick seaweed — all
this seemed to the wilted men in the touring car like an
oasis in the midst of a suffocating desert. The thin,
freckled, studious-looking youth with the wire spectacles
and the red bandanna, who was the driver, took a deep
breath of the moist air which had suddenly become
fresh and sweet. The bull-necked young deputy in the
rear seat sat up with a grunt and blinked his jet-black,
handsome eyes like a baby awakening from sleep. His
boyish, chubby, thick-witted face had a look of simple

astonishment on it as though never before had he en-
countered so pleasant a place. And the third man in
the car, Sheriff Tuckahue, unhitched his immense, an-
gular body from the crooked position into which it had
slumped and slowly raised his head from his chest,
looking like some strange, spiny, underwater animal
rising from the sea.

The car was still a little distance from the concrete
drive that curved up to the Smallwood home. Sheriff
Tuckahue leaned forward and jabbed the young driver
in the shoulder with a bony forefinger. "Pull up a minute, Charlie," he ordered.

The car stopped under the shade of one of the
overhanging willows. "We'll set heah a minute," the
sheriff said. He had a dry, hoarse, whiskey voice and
a curious way of talking with his thin lips pressed together and with the words sort of escaping from the
side of his mouth; he spoke as though he begrudged
the effort.

Harrison Towne, the barrel-bodied, bull-necked
deputy, was twenty-eight years old and looked like an
overgrown, high school football player. Now he labor-
iously mopped his porky, sweating face and swore softly
with the exaggerated emphasis that boys use when they
squat around in a circle smoking and spitting and
magnifying their toughness in each other's eyes. "Jesus!"
he exclaimed. "Jeeee — zus! Am ah broiled? Do ah
feel baked? Sam," he observed to the sheriff, "you could
fry an aig on me without crackin' the shell. Ah'm the
clostest thing to a boiled porgy you evah seen." He

turned around and slammed Charlie Rentle, the driver, on the shoulder with a beefy paw. "How are *you,* Charlie Wally?"

"Cut it out," Rentle said in a whining voice. "It's hot enough as it is."

"Charlie Wally's hot," Harrison said. "Charlie Wally's all bothered." He ruffled Rentle's thin, blond hair; his stubby forefingers dug hard into the youth's scalp.

"For Chrissakes, cut it out," Rentle said irritatedly. He jerked his head away.

Towne laughed. "Ah'm givin' you a free massage, Charlie. You don't want *all* that hair t'fall out?" He continued to laugh with exaggerated amusement. His laughter had a kind of snicker to it, a sort of loose, lewd quality as though anything he found amusing possessed some secret, smutty overtone. He glanced back at the sheriff to observe whether or not the clowning was appreciated. Sheriff Tuckahue was busy. He was uncorking his morning measure of rye whiskey.

During the ten years that Sam Tuckahue had remained Sheriff of Clarabell County, after giving up cotton raising for the steady income of a government office, his monthly salary had gone one-half in room and board to his widowed sister and one-half to rye whiskey. No one had ever seen him when he didn't have any liquor inside of him and no one had ever seen him completely drunk. He seemed to stay at a precise, well-calculated point of saturation.

Now, with a practiced movement of his tongue,

the sheriff dug a cud of tobacco from the pocket of his jaw and spit it accurately into the ditch. When about a quarter of the pint of whiskey had poured down his throat like sparkling water, he raised the bottle slowly from his lips and uttered a long, drawn out "Aaaaaaaah" of satisfaction. His upper lip puckered like the lip of a whinnying horse and for a moment his yellow, snaggy teeth were visible. Then he clamped his lips together again.

The sheriff was a tall man, considerably over six feet, with arms and legs like hickory fence rails. He was forty-five years old but looked fifty. Low down on his flat body he carried a round, little potbelly like a small beer keg. It looked incongruous in a man so devoid of flesh, but whenever Tuckahue referred to it his horse face would wrinkle with pleasure and he would explain carefully that there was six-thousand dollars of good rye whiskey in that cooking kettle if there was a single penny; and then he would thump on it.

Now, when he had corked the bottle, the sheriff bit off a chew of apple plug and leaned forward closer to the boy in the driver's seat. "Charlie," he said gently and amiably, through tight lips, "Charlie, you're the Gawd damdest driver ah evah seen. You make a car bounce like a mule with a bellyache."

"You told me to speed it up, didn't you?" Charlie argued with weary complaint in his voice. Whenever Tuckahue began this way, Charlie knew how it would continue.

"But ah didn't tell you to choose out every hole

in the road," the sheriff replied, warming up to the subject. "Gawd damn you, boy, you'd shake the best parts off a brass monkey."

"Ah'm sorry, Uncle Sam," Charlie apologized. He was new on this job and anxious to avoid trouble.

"Uncle? Jesus Christ, Uncle?" Tuckahue paused to draw a deep, wheezing, astonished breath. "Ain't ah told you nevah t'call me uncle? What you tryin' t'do, embarrass me before mah chief deppity? Mr. Rentle," he continued in an attitude of cold, pleasurable appraisal, "ah'll tell you what you are: You're a sway-backed, castrated, female bookkeeper. Mah good sister — may she die from a cancer in her private parts — " Deputy Towne haw-hawed, — "mah good sister must have had you all by herself. Or else, by Gawd, you couldna turned out like you did." Tuckahue slammed his palm down on the upholstery. "That's it, by Gawd. An' if you'd take your pants off, we'd find out ah'm dead right."

"How about it?" Deputy Towne suggested in a rapture at the idea.

"Ah nevah thought," the sheriff reflected, "ah nevah thought ah'd have a female bookkeeper for one of mah paid deppities. If it wasn't for the duty ah owe to mah kin . . . " he paused, unable to go on, gesturing melodramatically to indicate his misfortune.

"Ah reckon we better be goin' in to Mr. Smallwood," Rentle said wearily. "He'll git fussed up if we're late."

The sheriff's face turned sour. "Let him *git*," he said. His upper lip puckered. "*Mr.* Smallwood, Mr.

Avery J. Smallwood, prize bastard of the well known Smallwoods." He spit contemptuously into the ditch.

"Hell, let's stay here," offered Harrison Towne. "Let's stay right here till next winter. Hell, *it's hot*."

"Sure is hot," Rentle murmured. "We don't git rain pretty soon, cotton'll burn right off the ground."

"Hot! You're hot, eh?" the sheriff said. "Listen to him," he smirked aloud to the empty air, "he's hot! . . . Mr. Rentle, ah reckon ah'm just gonna fire you. Ah'm gonna fire you an' let you get a niggah job choppin' cotton all day. That'll learn you what's hot, Mr. Rentle."

There was a brief pause during which Rentle's peaked face became spotty with anger. Suddenly, as though arriving at a decision, he sat erect. He removed his wire spectacles. "Uncle Sam, ah'm tired of your talk," he said firmly. "You ain't gonna fire me. No, you won't!" He took a deep breath. His pale lids were winking against the sun. "All this hogwash about helpin' your kin. Ah been talkin' to mah maw . . . Ah found out about that dicker you made." His voice brimmed over with scorn. "You been gettin' free board since you took me on. An' that's the *only* reason you took me. You just favor that extra barrel of wildcat each month . . . Well, ah don't like you either, Uncle Sam," he said with sudden relish. "Soon as ah get a job in mah own line, ah'm gonna quit you. An' ah reckon when ah do, mah Uncle Sam'll come crawlin' on his knees beggin' me t'stay — cause he wants his extra whiskey. But ah reckon ah won't stay." Rentle's thin lips curved in a pleased smile. "Nooo! Ah reckon ah'll just tell you to go to hell. So you just stop your gassin', Uncle Sam, 'cause it don't make no difference . . ." This said, Rentle became occupied in polishing his spectacles.

Sheriff Tuckahue stared at the youth. For a moment his leathery, horse face was expressionless. Then, slowly, it commenced to wrinkle with amusement. The small, sharp eyes, which were green, and set far back in their bony sockets, glittered like bright, little stones. The upper lip puckered showing the yellow teeth. "That's right, Charlie," Tuckahue agreed softly in a curious, pleasurable tone of assent, "it *don't* make no difference." His eyes sparkled. "An' ah'll tell you somethin' else: when the time comes, Charlie, ah'm *gonna* crawl to you. Yessir! You know why?" He burst out into a short, fierce cry of pleasure and malice. " 'Cause ah'm a smart man! When there's somethin' ah want, ah'll do anythin' t'get it — ah'll even *crawl* for it. Yessir!" His voice boomed out: "Money talks, Charlie, money talks! An' a smart man crawls before them that's got it!" The sheriff reached for his whiskey bottle. He drank greedily. After a moment he clamped his lips together in a tight, malicious smile. "Ah've kept mah job by givin' money to the right places. Yessir! An' ah've *used* mah job t' *take* money from the right places. Yessir! Ah've licked the right boots an' had mah boots licked by them who depends on me. *Yessir!* Ain't that right, Mr. Towne?"

"Sure is," Towne said laughing.

"You lick mah boots whenever ah snap mah little finger, don't you, Mr. Towne?"

"Sure do," the deputy laughed.

"An' that's the way it's *gotta* be," the sheriff concluded proudly. "That's the way of things! But it takes a smart man to know it. Ah know it!" he said looking at the others in triumph, "ah know it!" He gulped down another two fingers of whiskey. "Look at that," he ordered, pointing to the lawn in front of the Smallwood home where half-a-dozen fat sheep were stepping slowly in the shade. "That's what the Smallwoods can do!" "The Smallwoods can keep sheep just to crop their Gawd damn lawns. But *we* can't do that," he demonstrated in venomous triumph, "we can't do that!" He tilted his bottle and then started speaking while the liquor still gurgled down his throat. " 'Bring two deppities, Mr. Tuckahue!' he says to me. 'What's the mattah, Mr. Smallwood?' ah asks. 'About twelve o'clock,' he answers me." Tuckahue glared at his two deputies. "What kind of an answer is that?"

The two deputies didn't reply.

"So ah goes out on a Sunday — on a Sunday, mind you — an' ah drives all the way down heah with mah nephew Charlie Bonehead at the wheel, an' Mr. Smallwood'll say to me: 'Mr. Tuckahue,' he'll say, 'ah want you to scratch mah back!' An' what'll ah do?" The sheriff paused with his little eyes gleaming like bright stones. "Why ah'll scratch his back," he said with bitter relish. "Ah'll scratch any Gawd damn part of him he wants," he finished off in triumph. "Because he's Mr. Avery J. Smallwood an' he owns ten-thousand acres an' a thousand niggahs an' ah'll do just what he says like ah was a niggah mahself — because mah good job depends on it. *Yessir!*" Tuckahue slammed his palm down with a smart crack on his bony knee. "Ah'll walk me up to Mr. Smallwood an' ah'll knuckle me down an' scrape mah belly an' Mr. Smallwood'll say: *'there's* a good man. He knows *his place* all right. Ah sure need him in that *sheriff's* job!' " Tuckahue snorted happily. He pounded the upholstery. "By Gawd if ah won't scrape me down just like a niggah sharecropper."

The sheriff jumped to his feet. He put on his long, black preacher's coat. "C'mon, Charlie," he bellowed, "bounce this car. Ah got a need t'do me some scrapin'!"

II

The Smallwood home was modern in style and elegantly handsome in its setting of green shrubs, leafy trees and delicately designed flower beds. It was the only house of its kind in a district where the majority of planters had not even been able to touch paint to their old homes for five years past, let alone build new ones. As such it was both a showplace and a source of burning envy. By continuing to prosper through the lean years of the cotton market, Avery Smallwood had been almost unique in the owning class of his district. Malice dismissed him as lucky, but there was sound enterprise behind his success. His plantation was unusually large, for one thing; he ginned his own cotton, for another; and most important, he controlled a weave

mill in Baton Rouge which bought the cotton he himself sold. These things had enabled him to push ahead
where so many others had gone under.

All of this — the house and the well-kept grounds,
the fruit orchard which extended for a mile before the
cotton fields began again, the new brick garage with
servants' quarters overhead, the grazing meadows, the
flowers, the trees, — were a very special sight in the
surrounding sea of tumbledown shacks and naked cotton fields. No visitor ever left Clarabell County without first driving past the Smallwood plantation.

Now, on this hot Sunday morning, as the open
touring car with the three deputies swung up the long
driveway, Avery Smallwood turned from his work on
the veranda to see who was there. He had been hard
at his painting since nine o'clock. When he caught sight
of Tuckahue's dark, spiny figure jouncing in the rear
seat, a grimace of disgust crossed his face and he turned
back to his canvas. Smallwood didn't like Tuckahue.
He never had. With great care he stippled a spot of
color onto his canvas. He stepped away. Then he
frowned. It was no good — it was no good at all. He
sighed impatiently. Nothing he had done that morning
was worth the time he had spent on it. He would have
been much better off playing with the children. And
now Tuckahue was coming.

Smallwood sighed again. He was a small man,
only a little over five feet, with delicate, handsome features and a rather stern cast to his dark face. It was a
bitter thing in his life, and it always had been, that he
was physically so puny. He had never quite accepted

it, as he had never quite accepted other aspects of his life. Unconsciously now, as though he were still a boy, ashamed before other boys, the image of Tuckahue loomed up before him — a big, ugly, yellow-toothed ape, ostentatiously bending over, indicating by a sly, little smirk that he was only trying to hear a little better . . . Aaaah, Smallwood thought, life had always been like that. It never seemed to offer a complete, a wholehearted satisfaction; success never came but it carried some gripe of defeat. As a boy there was his size. Now there was his work. And other things.

His work! What was his work? Smallwood asked himself the question now, as he had done many times before. Was his work business or painting? After college he had studied painting in Europe for a few years. He had returned home just before his father's death and taken over the management of the plantation. Taken it over successfully. Improved it; built a cotton gin; bought control in a mill. He was a successful man. He had a pretty wife whom he loved, he had children who were fine, bright, excellent youngsters — was he happy? No. Had he ever been truly happy, truly satisfied with life? No. Never. And what was it? He didn't know. He never could find the answer. He only knew that something which pleased him on Wednesday would weary him on Friday. At the age of thirty-eight, when he had more responsibilities than he had ever had, and more success, he had gone back to his painting. Three days each week now he hurried home from Baton Rouge to spend all day on the shady veranda with his oils and his canvas. Well, he knew one thing: In those hours spent at painting he was able to forget what some people called commerce and what he knew to be a dirty business of "grasp and grab" — he was able to relax sufficiently to go back to that dirty business on the following week. Now, as many times before, Smallwood asked himself why he didn't retire. He smiled faintly to himself by way of answer. He knew why! He was afraid! Who could guarantee that painting wouldn't come to weary him as much as business? And besides he was frank enough to admit that he needed the success of his business life, he needed the sense of achievement that success brought him. Well, it was a compromise! His soul, God bless it, seemed to be divided; he might as well divide his life. Nothing was completely satisfactory; a man had to take what he could. If he'd been like other men, he might have turned to travel, or to women, or to drink. How many men he knew were doing that — trying to buy with money the satisfactions they lacked. No, that wasn't his way. There were too many pigs in the world already. He needn't add himself.

But this Bailey business. Smallwood shook his head, in a stir of irritation. Just when he wanted to be by himself, he had to put his mind to a stupid affair that never should have occurred in the first place. But there was Ed Bailey, howling in bed over a broken jaw, and the nigrah boy Beecher under lock and key in the cellar. Well, there was no way out of it — he could see that. But it had to be handled properly. No brutality. There was going to be no nigrah beating or lynch parties for a boy of his.

The touring car with the three deputies in it came to a stop. Smallwood turned his back and pretended to be absorbed in his painting. He pictured Tuckahue standing before him — a big, snaggle-toothed ape with his tongue hanging out and his little, pig eyes hunting around for a mouthful of liquor. All right — he could look. He could look till he got blue in the face. A man had the right to expect the hospitality of a drink but Tuckahue was a god-damn sponge. Give him a taste of some good liquor and he'd stick like a burr till he had sopped it all up. And Smallwood wanted to get back to his painting. If that damn fool Bailey had only kept his hands where they belonged, or if that Beecher boy had only been off somewhere in a card game — aaaaaah, now the whole plantation would be in a bad humor for weeks and work would fall off just when the cotton needed most care. The blacks were like that — get them upset over something and they popped off like a lot of children . . . Smallwood heard the clump of Tuckahue's brogans as the sheriff mounted the steps. He wished he hadn't come so soon.

But it had to be done. You couldn't overlook it when a nigrah hit a white man.

III

Sheriff Tuckahue left his two deputies sitting in the car and went up to the veranda alone. Smallwood's back was turned to him. The sheriff smirked with contempt as Smallwood delicately applied a pinpoint of color to the canvas. What a friggin' little rooster this Smallwood was; what a friggin' little ass with his double heels and his "ain't I la de la?" painting . . .

"Good mawnin', Mr. Smallwood," Tuckahue said aloud in a practiced, hearty voice. "It sure is a pleasure seein' you again."

"Eh?" Smallwood turned around. He affected surprise. "Oh! — Good morning to you. Excuse me, ah didn't hear your car come in. How are you?" He held out his hand. He gave the sheriff's stringy, sweating paw a short, gingerish shake with his own small hand, and quickly withdrew it again.

"Jim Dandy," the sheriff replied . . . "Ah see you're doin' your pictures again," he observed, smiling.

"Why yes!" Smallwood looked up at Tuckahue with a faint, malicious curve on his full lips. "How do you like it?"

The sheriff's eyelids flickered. He knew this game. If he didn't step back fast, the little bastard'd have him floundering around like a horse in quicksand.

"Ah'd be grateful t'know what you think," Smallwood said softly. His voice was liquid, easy. There was no suspicion of irony in his polished tone.

Tuckahue studied the canvas. It was a highly impressionist representation of a cow with a young calf suckling at its teat. The sheriff blinked his eyes. He couldn't make head or tail out of the damn thing. Falteringly he turned to Smallwood with a smile that was meant to be ingratiating. "Pshaw, Mr. Smallwood,

ah like it fine, but ah reckon *ah* don't know anythin'
about sich matters . . ." That oughta hold him, he
thought. He don't get no fish bait outa me.

"An' how do you like the color of the cow, Mr.
Tuckahue?"

"The — the cow?" Tuckahue stammered.

Smallwood nodded.

Tuckahue studied the painting again. The cow was
lemon green on a blue background. He swore softly to
himself. "Fine, Mr. Smallwood, looks fine to me."

"Did you evah see a cow like that?" Smallwood
inquired softly.

The sheriff cleared his throat several times before
speaking. He wished he had a drink. "Reckon ah didn't,
Mr. Smallwood. But, shucks, ah don't know anythin'
about pictures," he added hastily. The bastard, he murmured to himself, the little bastard.

"No, ah guess it isn't very real," Smallwood observed, as though it had never occurred to him before.
"Do you feel ah ought to change it?"

"Why, shucks, Mr. Smallwood, ah don't know."

Smallwood looked up at Tuckahue's tight, un-
comfortable face. His lips twitched with suppressed
amusement. Then abruptly he tired of it. It was like
baiting a hulk of wood. "Have a chair, Mr. Tuckahue,"
he said. "We'll get to business."

A slight, uncontrollable sigh of relief issued from
the sheriff's lips. He sat down quickly and folded his
loose, stringy hands in his lap. He wished for a drink
but he knew it wouldn't do to take his own. He hoped
Smallwood would offer him some.

Smallwood picked up his palette and began squeezing little dabs of paint onto the edge. He mixed the paint slowly with a small, fine brush. Finally he spoke: "We had some trouble out heah last night . . . A nigrah boy slugged Mr. Bailey. Broke his jaw."

"You don't mean to tell me?" Tuckahue's voice was startled but his lips remained tight. He sat up in his chair.

"Mr. Bailey's bad off," Smallwood continued in his soft, even, polished tone. "I have a doctor on him. He'll have to chew milk for three months."

"You don't say? . . . Jiminy," the sheriff reflected, "that musta been a mean niggah. You don't break Ed Bailey's jaw easy. Or did the niggah use a rock?"

Smallwood shook his head. "Nooooo — no mean nigrah at all. An' he didn't use anything, 'cause ah saw his hand. George Beecher's his name."

"Don't know him," the sheriff murmured.

"Well . . ." Smallwood paused for a moment with his dark, handsome head bent over the palette ". . . Ah reckon he had cause." He sighed wearily. "Mr. Bailey got liquored up last night . . . went after a little yaller girl ovah by the orchard . . . she didn't want him — guess she was too young anyway . . . well . . . that's how it started . . ."

Tuckahue sat back in his chair. A sly grin played at the corners of his mouth. He knew Big Ed Bailey; he coveted Bailey's job. The man who was head riding boss for Avery Smallwood had the best spot in four counties. A thing like this might see Bailey out. "Ah reckon it ain't the first time," Tuckahue said slowly, enjoying himself. "When they start gettin' old as fo'-teen, Ed don't like 'em no more." The sly, lewd grin crinkled the corners of his mouth. His little, flinty eyes danced. He hooked a thumb under one suspender and looked closely at Smallwood, calculating the effect of his remark. "Nooo," he added as a kind of casual after-thought, "ah reckon it won't be the last time either. Ed Bailey's just naturally got a taste for pullets."

Smallwood turned his head away. Tuckahue disgusted him. Licking his chops over a business like this. The leering and the nice, sly little pointers . . . Good God — the realization struck Smallwood suddenly — Tuckahue wanted the job for himself. Well — he smiled inwardly. Before he'd hire a sponge like Tuckahue for his personal manager, he'd give up cotton growing. But it wasn't so funny. Getting too big for himself that man . . . Smallwood squeezed a tube of paint delicately between thumb and forefinger . . . might be time he was kicked out of the sheriff's office. No — Smallwood checked himself — couldn't say he wasn't a good blood-hound. Well — let him stay there — so long as he kept in his place. He chuckled over the image. A blood-hound was correct. Give Mista Sheriff a pair of flop ears an' he'd look fine for a bloodhound.

Smallwood turned and presented a friendly countenance to the sheriff. His tone was suave: "Ah reckon it's too bad about Bailey. But he's the best manager ah evah had. Keeps the riding bosses on the job, keeps the nigrahs from lazin', takes care of everything now ah'm away so much . . . Ah reckon ah ought to give him another chance."

Tuckahue licked his lips with the edge of his tongue. He leaned forward. "Ah reckon ah wouldn't be a good friend of yours, Mr. Smallwood, if ah didn't advise you that poor Ed Bailey just can't help himself. He'll promise all right — but you'll just have the same thing all ovah . . ." Tuckahue waited.

"Well — ah suppose ah'll be forced to get rid of him then," Smallwood admitted regretfully. "But he's an awful efficient man."

Tuckahue ran his tongue around the outside of his lips again. Then he plunged: "Mr. Smallwood, ah don't mind sayin' frankly that ah'd sure like to be in Ed Bailey's shoes. It'd be a real pleasure to work for you, Mr. Smallwood."

"Well!" Smallwood's smile was friendly. "It's good to know that, Mr. Tuckahue. Ah'll have to think it ovah."

"That's fine, Mr. Smallwood, that's Jim Dandy." Tuckahue's little eyes sparkled. By Gawd he said to himself, by Gawd, by Gawd!

"Of course," Smallwood remarked with a worried air, "ah understand you don't work any more unless you have your nephew, Charlie Rentle, on salary too . . . Ah'm afraid ah couldn't afford the both of you," he submitted apologetically.

Tuckahue's face flushed a copper red. "Why no sich thing, Mr. Smallwood," he protested, "wherever did you hear that?"

Smallwood shrugged grievingly.

"Why no sich thing," Tuckahue repeated. "Ah put that boy on 'cause he's smart, that's all. Best deppity ah've got. Just a lot of loose tongues flappin', Mr. Smallwood."

Smallwood smiled. "Well, ah reckon ah better keep Mr. Bailey on for a piece. At least he grows cotton for me. If *you* was mah manager, mah only crop'd be corn mash!" Smallwood burst into laughter. He found it impossible to contain himself. The sheriff's face was as long as a cornstalk. An incredible ass. Imagine him taking Bailey's job. And thinking he could do it too.

Tuckahue joined in the laughter. He forced a series of weak, little chuckles out of the side of his tight mouth and then lapsed into silence. His eyes were brilliant with hatred.

Smallwood got over his amusement. "This is what I want done with the nigrah boy," he said.

Tuckahue listened with his long, horse head turned away. He felt choked inside. He wanted to reach out. He wanted Smallwood by the throat for just one little minute. He'd break him in two. He'd break the little bastard in two.

"Ah want some of the starch taken out of Beecher," Smallwood said. "We just can't let him feel he can raise his hand like that and go free as a sparrow. For his own good he's got to be taught."

"It ain't the first niggah ah've perked up with a little pistol whupping," the sheriff said sullenly. "Ah'll better him ovah night."

"No you don't!" Smallwood's voice was sharp. "That's just what ah don't want!"

Well say what you want, goddamit, Tuckahue raged to himself. What the hell am I supposed to do, guess it? . . . "You want him on the road gang for a spell?" he asked with terrific restraint.

"Noooo — " Smallwood pursed his lips. "Ah reckon not. Beecher's a good hand. Mah cotton needs a lot of carin' for right now. Sun's makin' the weeds shoot up smart. No-o-o, ah reckon if he's just scared some, it'll do fine. That's why ah didn't want you down heah alone. It'll put a fear of the law in him to see some deputies."

So that was why! A sheriff and two deputies to come all the way down here to scare a lone niggah. Because Smallwood wanted it that way. Tuckahue squirted tobacco juice angrily over the porch rail.

"Be careful of them flowers, Mr. Tuckahue," Smallwood said. "You'll have mah wife on your neck . . . Tell you what you do," he went on, "you take Beecher an' set him in the worst cell you got. Don't give him no bed to sleep on. Give him a plate of slop once a day that'll turn his stomach. And just forget about him. Ah reckon after he sits hungry and thirsty for a couple days, he'll come back heah and think it's Paradise. He'll think twice before he hits a white man again . . ." Smallwood paused. "You know, ah don't like to do this," he added earnestly. "But it's sure for the boy's own good. He don't learn now, he'll learn it bitter some other day. That's true, ain't it?"

Tuckahue nodded.

Smallwood took a key from his pocket. "Have one of your men bring him up heah, will you?" he asked. "He's in the cellar — around to the back. Ah want to speak to him first."

Tuckahue went down to the car and gave the key to Deputy Towne. They talked together for a moment. Towne lumbered off behind the house. As Tuckahue returned he suddenly removed his hat with an exaggerated flourish. A woman stepped out on the veranda. It was Mrs. Smallwood. She gave the sheriff a friendly but puzzled little "how do," which instantly enraged him, and he watched her with an acid twist to his mouth as she swung down toward her husband. She was a supple, athletic woman of thirty with a pretty, placid face. She walked firmly with neat haunches swaying and her ripe, prominent breasts jouncing softly beneath her knitted dress. "Hello, Avy," she said as she came up to Smallwood, "what have you done with George?" She bent and kissed him on the cheek. She was several inches taller than he. Her voice was charming, full and vibrant with a singing lilt to it. It fitted her fine body.

Smallwood touched her shoulder in a light, caressing gesture. "Just get up?"

"Yes." She laughed deliciously. "Aren't I awful? Avy, you're not going to put him on that awful chain gang, are you?" she asked seriously.

Smallwood shook his head. "Mr. Tuckahue's just going to let him cool down for a few days."

"Oh!" She swung around to the sheriff. "How do, Mr. Tuckahue?" The sheriff bowed a little. It was obvious that she hadn't recognized him and it burned him up. He had been introduced to her three or four times already.

"Promise me you won't hurt him?"

"Certainly not, ma'm."

"Ah'll nevah forgive you if you do," she said, smiling warmly at him, displaying her even, white, little teeth.

"Don't worry, ma'm," Tuckahue assured her. "A niggah boy's like a setter dog. Train him right an' he'll be all right."

"Ah think it's just awful what happened. Avy promised me he could be mah chauffeur when cotton season was ovah. Ah was countin' on it."

"Well, if he behaves himself," Smallwood said. "We'll see about it."

"Thank you, Avy. He's an awful cute boy. Ah'm countin' on havin' him."

"All right, dear." Smallwood touched her shoulder again in the same light, caressing gesture. The pleasure he took in her was patent on his face. "He's coming out now. Ah need to talk to him."

"Can't ah stay?" She smiled prettily at him like a child begging for a favor.

"No, dear."

"Oh." She made a little grimace. Then she laughed. "Ah wish ah was a man. Ah think it's awful bein' a woman, don't you, sheriff?"

Tuckahue grunted. He tried hard to find something gallant to say but the words stuck in his throat. He grunted again.

Mrs. Smallwood looked at the sheriff with veiled amusement. She gave a little bird laugh that trilled in her throat. "Now don't you hurt him," she said. She swung down the porch with her soft, jouncing, beautiful stride.

The men watched her. They were silent for a moment.

She went inside.

IV

George Beecher stretched his cramped body and wondered what time it was. He was hungry and he had been for several hours. The fine, brown dust in the cellar, which had been blowing in from the dry fields all month, was thick in his throat. It ached him to swallow.

He stood up when he heard the heavy door being unbolted. It's heah, he thought. A slight pain stabbed the swollen knuckles of his right hand. He waited nervously.

"Hey you!" Deputy Towne's voice boomed down into the cellar. "Hey you there — come on up!"

Beecher moved slowly with scraping shoes toward the shaft of light that slanted down the wooden stairway.

"Hey there, niggah, you deaf or you drunk? Come on, up."

"Ah'm comin'," Beecher said.

"You're mighty goddam slow about it."

"It dark in heah, boss."

Beecher reached the stairway and mounted it slowly. It's heah, he said to himself again.

Deputy Towne stepped back from the doorway as
Beecher came up. Then he laughed and dropped his
hand from his revolver. "Shucks," he said, "ah thought
you was a man-eatin' tiger. You sure you the boy ah
want?"

"Ah reckon so, Captain."

"Well come on then, Mr. Smallwood wants to see
you."

It's heah, Beecher said to himself once more.

They walked side by side around the house.

"What the hell's the mattah with you, boy?"
Towne asked curiously. "You drunk last night?"

"Nossuh, boss."

"You sure had *some* kind of devil in you."

Beecher didn't answer. His feet scraped the gravel.
He put his swollen hand carefully into the pocket of
his overalls.

"You don't give a damn, do you?" Towne said
with amused contempt. "Just a ba — ad niggah, don't
care what happens to you?"

Beecher saw Mr. Smallwood on the porch talking
to Sheriff Tuckahue. He saw the touring car parked on
the driveway with another white deputy in it. He
walked forward and a slow, throbbing flow surged up
hot and bitter in his body. Inside him a voice was
whispering, speaking to him. It didn't seem like his own
voice. It was deep inside, buried deep down. It kept
repeating itself like a record on a talking machine, over
again, over again: "That's it, white deppity, that's it,
that's it . . ." He felt strange. It was strange to have a
voice inside you and you walking meanwhile, listening

to it. "That's it, white deppity. Don't care whut happen. Got a bellyfull of carin'. Can't eat carin' no more. That's it, white deppity."

"Go on up, boy," Towne said. He remained on the gravel driveway.

Beecher mounted the steps. He walked mechanically, a little like a man abstracted. Deep inside him the steady whisper kept repeating itself. He heard it, strange, like a buzz saw hidden in a wood. Then he saw the white men turn. They were looking at him. His head lifted a little. He didn't know it. He didn't know he had lifted his head. He walked slowly, facing them. It's heah now; he said it to himself quietly; heah now. His feet were heavy.

V

When Sheriff Tuckahue heard Beecher coming up the steps, he turned to look at him. He was surprised. He had expected a much bigger man. Beecher was middling in height, rather thin. He looked about twenty-two. His face and his naked shoulders and arms were coffee-brown. Tuckahue could see why the Mrs. wanted him for a chauffeur. He had a nice, pleasing, smooth-skinned face, not one of those ape-looking fellers. Still, Tuckahue reflected, there was something bad about the boy's eye. By God now if it didn't look like Beecher had a "notion" in his eye. Yessir. That was it, all right.

He could see it now. Well — Tuckahue stroked his nose. He felt a little upset. A nice looking niggah boy like that with a notion in his eye. And you could always tell it. Dogs and horses were the same. You had to catch 'em quick or they went bad. Well, he'd catch him. He'd take that notion out of him quicker'n a pig could whistle. It wouldn't be the first time.

"Come on ovah, George," Mr. Smallwood said.

Beecher moved closer to the white men. Smallwood sat down and dangled one leg over the arm of his chair. He felt nervous now that the boy was standing in front of him. Punishing Beecher was easy. Too easy! Any brute could do it. What he had to do was make him understand what he ran into when he hit a white man. Like teaching a child what reality was like. It wasn't simple.

Smallwood surveyed the youth quietly for a moment. Then seriously, earnestly, in his liquid, even tone he said, "Well, George, how do you feel about what happened last night?"

Beecher didn't reply. His eyes were cast down a little. He was looking at Smallwood's leg dangling over the edge of the chair. The leg swung back and forth in a little arc and Beecher followed it with his eye, following the white shoe. His throat felt choked with sand. He wondered if he could ask for some water.

"Did you hear me, George?"

"Yes, boss." The youth answered in a low, hoarse, guttural tone.

Tuckahue nodded a little. He knew the tone too. The tone and the eye went together. You could tell the

stubbornness in them, like a hard wall that wouldn't
be moved.

"Don't call me 'boss' George," Smallwood said.
"Call me Mr. Smallwood." He paused for a moment,
scrutinizing him . . . "Are you sorry for what you
did, George?"

Beecher turned his eyes away from Smallwood's
probing glance. He started to talk, stopped. Then he
cleared his throat and swallowed. "Whut you *want* me
t'do, Mista Smallwood?"

Quietly, inflexibly, Smallwood repeated his question. "Are you sorry for what you did? I want you to
answer me, George."

There was a moment of silence. Then Beecher
raised his head. Inside him there was pride and fear
and fierce determination. "Nossuh! Ah do it again!
Niggah get lynched for what Bailey done!"

"Niggah get lynched for what you do," Tuckahue
broke in harshly. He sluiced a stream of tobacco over
the porch rail. "What's the mattah with you, boy,
talkin' like that? What you do, an' what a white man
does, is two hell of a different things. An' don't you
evah forget it!"

Beecher turned his head. His face was sullen,
smoldering; all twenty-two years of his life were running hot and bitter into this one moment, pumping in
his body like a flood tide. Inside him there was a torrent
of rebellion, and blind, unheeding determination to
speak out. He was engulfed by it. "You want ah let
him force that little girl?" he cried in a passionate burst
of speech. "She no more'n ten year old."

Tuckahue started to answer. Smallwood interrupted him. "Mr. Tuckahue," he remarked acidly, "ah'd like to remind you, for the second time, not to spit juice on mah wife's flowers."

"Excuse me," Tuckahue stammered. By God, he raged to himself, ah'd give a month's liquor to drive a boar pig right through those goddam flowers.

"You shouldn't have hit him," Smallwood said to Beecher.

Beecher took a step forward. His face became distorted with emotion and pleading. "Whut *could* ah do, boss? Ah *tell* him get away! He don't care *whut* ah say. Ah gotta do *somep'n,* don't I? When ah pull him off, he hit me, knock me down. Second time ah hit him back. Whut you *want* me t'do?"

Smallwood jumped to his feet. "Ah want you to know enough not to hit a white man," he shouted angrily. "You should have run for help, or yelled, or done something like that — but you shouldn't have hit him!"

Beecher stood silent, trembling, face to face with Smallwood. His eyes were brilliant, blazing with emotion. A reckless, overwhelming desire to lash back at this white man was pulsing in his throat: to speak out once, to speak free, to raise his face once from the black earth and look free at a blue sky, to raise his head proud like a free bird flying — it choked him. He couldn't speak.

Abruptly Smallwood sat down. He wiped his brow with a handkerchief. He felt irritated with himself. He had lost his temper and he shouldn't have. But, God

— the boy was incredible. He couldn't see a step
beyond his own nose. Where did he think he was —
in Mars or in Clarabell County, Louisiana? By God,
he didn't have the faintest recognition of a nigrah's position in the south. Talking like he was a nigrah chief
back in Africa. Well he wasn't, he was a black boy in
a white man's world. He'd ruin himself forever that
way . . . And one thing was decided: Beecher would
stay at farm work and stay close. A chauffeur's job
would ruin him for good.

"George," Smallwood said more quietly, "you
just forget about Mr. Bailey. He's mah job, not yours.
What you've got to see is what *you* did. Nigrahs have
been lynched for hitting a white man — and you know
it. Ah'll take care of Mr. Bailey."

"How?" The word came in a whisper. Beecher's
body was bent over, rigid; his burning, bloodshot eyes
were fixed on Smallwood's face. He had lost control
of himself. His whole being was engulfed by blind out-
rage at this white man's world. Through this one moment his whole life was speaking. It was twenty-two
years of being a sharecropper; it was the long rising
water breaking over the levee; the deep, cumulative
torrent hammering at last on the stone wall of flesh
and custom, of gun and whip. "How?" he repeated.
"How? How? How you take keer of him? You gonna
send him to a chain gang? You gonna try him in a
niggah court like you stand me up in a white man's?"

Smallwood flushed. His breathing became noisy.
Then he gave a curious, little laugh and when his voice
came it was strange, with a kind of breathless restraint.

"Bailey's not your business, George! Ah told you that! Ah'll tend to Bailey!"

"Sure you tend to Bailey!!!" Beecher's body snapped erect. The lifetime of scorn and bitterness, of suffering and injustice, poured out of him in a hysterical, reckless outburst. "You talk sweet but you *do* like all the rest! You gone put me on a chain gang but *he* ain't gone be there! You *know* he ain't! *You just lyin'!*"

Smallwood struck him in the face. Beecher reeled back a step and then held his ground. "Go ahead," he cried hysterically, "you cain't hurt me. When ah bust that white man on the jaw ah did the best thing ah evah did in mah whole life. You cain't hurt me no more. Ah don't care whut you do!"

Smallwood stopped. His clenched hand was raised in the air. His dark face had turned sickly gray. He stood motionless, quivering, almost beyond self-control. But he stood still. He didn't strike again. And then, suddenly, a shiver passed through him, and in a quick, convulsive movement he brought his hand down to his chest. A look of strange, wild shame passed over his face. He was *wrong!* Jesus Christ, he was wrong! He *had* been lying. A nigrah boy had showed him for a liar.

Smallwood dropped into his chair. He clasped his head with both hands. His whole being felt agonized. Good God, how low he'd been to hit that boy. With all his fine words, how much like any other white planter, so quick to raise his hand, so keen for the rope!

He groaned. In that blind moment when Beecher had called him a liar, he had been dominated by an

impulse to kill. Now the madness was gone but in its
place there was a sense of physical pain that shot
through his body in long, burning streaks. Good God,
had all the years of his life been a lie too? It couldn't
be! No! *That moment* was a lie. Only that moment. He
was different from the other planters. He had shown
it. He had proven it.

The pain began to dwindle. He felt a little easier.
Yes, he was calmer now . . . No, no, he thought soberly,
it was obviously not true. He'd run this plantation for
ten years, and he'd run it without the brutality and
the gun rule that other planters used. And he hadn't
cheated. God knows he admitted that his nigrahs
didn't earn much more than their keep. They were
poverty-stricken and they'd never be anything else.
They lived in sties and they were herded around like
cattle. But the price of cotton did that, not him. He
had to compete or go out of business. The price of
cotton did that. But by God he didn't cheat them the
way the others did. He was no white, southern "gentle-
man" scaring up a lynching for a dull Saturday night.
No, and he wasn't going to be!

Smallwood took a deep breath. He looked at
Beecher. The boy was standing still, rigid, with his
head slightly bowed and with a kind of blank film over
his eyes. His mouth was open and he was drawing
great, panting breaths.

Small came to a decision: Bailey had to go! Yes,
that was the first thing! Christ, how conveniently his
mind had skipped over Bailey's part in the whole business. Bailey was useful to him and so he had been

prepared to give him another chance. Would he have given Beecher another chance if Beecher had tried to rape a white girl? Hardly. No, Bailey would go and go today. And it was only too bad he couldn't be put on trial. But there you ran up against the community. No other planter would stand for a white man on trial for the rape of a nigrah girl. It was out of the question. But Bailey would be out of a good job and that was something. But Beecher? Beecher? It was hard — but Beecher had to learn. The world was what it was — and you couldn't get away from it. A nigrah boy who thought he could strike a white man with impunity would end up one day on the limb of a tree. Better to teach him now as you teach a child that strikes its parent. And you couldn't reason with him any more than you could reason with a child. Punish him; make it as mild as possible, but make him learn the code of the world before he got in the way — and the world ran him down. It was too bad but it had to be done.

"George," Smallwood said in a low, restrained voice, "George, ah want to apologize to you!"

Now, after the long, excruciating silence that had gripped the porch, as Sheriff Tuckahue heard what Smallwood finally had to say, he cringed physically under the wave of nausea that struck in his stomach. He felt he would burst with rage. A moment before, when he had been listening to Beecher, he had felt closer to clubbing him down than any other niggah he had ever heard. He had checked himself, he was thankful for that. Beecher was Smallwood's niggah. The quickest way he could find himself out of a sheriff's job, and right back chopping cotton, was to stick a snoot into Smallwood's business. And so he had waited for what Smallwood would do. And now — God Almighty it was incredible — Avery Smallwood was apologizing to a niggah! Tuckahue straightened up. His thin lips tightened. He waited with cold contempt for what Smallwood would say.

And Beecher had stood waiting also! Inside him that strange voice, the voice that seemed to issue from a throat other than his own, that strange, low whisper out of another world, which he had never experienced until that moment when Deputy Towne, the sheriff's deputy, the white man's deputy, had come with the law swinging on his hip to unlock the cellar door and bring him out for punishment, until the moment when the bitter flow of twenty-two years of a black share-cropper's life had surged up madly through his worn, nervous body — inside him that voice murmured final and bitter, over and over again: "it's done; heah now; finished now!" And Beecher had waited. His throat felt choked and he had cried wildly to himself: "Don't care. Don't care. Ah don't care!"

And then Smallwood had sat down. The blow had not come; the whip lash had not ripped his back; the rope had not burned; Smallwood had sat down. And Beecher had said it. Twenty-two years had burst out. In one great moment he had said it and a thousand others with him. He had raised his head up proud like a free bird flying. It was all right now. It was all right!

"George," Smallwood said in a low, constrained

voice, "ah want to thank you for all you said. Ah was going to let Mr. Bailey off, but ah won't now. Ah'm gonna discharge him an' ah thank you for speaking up."

Tuckahue gritted his teeth together. It was the most amazing thing he had ever heard a planter say to a niggah . . . But it was none of his business. An' he sure wasn't going to get mixed up in it.

"Do you hear me, George?" Smallwood said, with his head bowed and his eyes fixed on the floor. It was hard for him to look at Beecher. He had made up his mind and he was carrying it through — but it was a hard thing to apologize like that, humble yourself, strip naked before an inferior. Yet, in spite of his shame, Smallwood had a curious feeling of happiness at the same time, a strange, troubled flush of pleasure at what he was doing. He knew it was right; he knew it was something no other planter would do — yet it cut hard . . . "Ah'm going to fire Mr. Bailey, George."

Beecher was silent.

Smallwood raised his head. "But you, George, you can't go on thinking you can hit a white man an' not suffer for it." His voice became louder. There was a note of firm resolve to it. "Ah'm sorry, George, but you've got to learn that. You've got to learn what this world's like we live in. If you don't learn, you'll end up on the limb of a tree. Ah wouldn't want that happening to you."

Smallwood paused. He commenced to swing his leg over the arm of his chair again. "Ah'll see the judge," he continued more softly. "Ah'll tell him what happened. Maybe he'll let you off easy. Ah hope so. But you got to learn what the world's like before you come back heah."

Smallwood fingered his paintbrush. He picked absently at a loose hair. "All right, Mr. Tuckahue," he said, and his voice once more found its even, liquid note. "You can take him now."

Sheriff Tuckahue jerked his head. "Get down to the car!" Beecher turned slowly and went off. He walked now as he had before with his head down, his feet scraping mechanically, his bruised hand in the pocket of his overalls. Deputy Towne met him at the stairs and took him by the arm.

Tuckahue sidled over to Smallwood. "You mean that about the judge?" he asked out of the corner of his mouth.

Smallwood shook his head. "No! You just keep him in jail. Let him stew. If he asks about a trial, you tell him the judge is on vacation. Ah'll keep in touch with you. Ah reckon it'll take longer than ah expected."

Tuckahue's upper lip puckered, "You give me a free hand with him, it won't take so long," he said.

Smallwood flushed. "Ah don't want you to touch him," he snapped. "You do as ah say!"

"Certainly, Mr. Smallwood, ah won't lift a finger to him." Tuckahue's contempt was so strong within him that Smallwood sensed it. He sensed it although the thin lips remained tight, and the sharp, bony face revealed nothing.

"Eh — just a moment, Mr. Tuckahue." Smallwood surveyed him amiably. "About Mr. Bailey's job . . ."

"Yes?" Tuckahue's little eyes lit up instantly.

"Ah'm afraid ah can't give it to you!"

"Oh!" It was an involuntary grunt.

"No, ah'm afraid not," Smallwood repeated smoothly. "But if you're tired of being sheriff, Mr. Tuckahue, ah reckon we could fix it. Might be your nephew could take it over."

"Why no, suh, no," Tuckahue stammered.

"Ah thought maybe you were tired of it."

"No sich thing, no sich thing, Mr. Smallwood! Why . . . why . . . you can ask anybody," Tuckahue stammered. "Don't ah do mah job? You ain't had any trouble with me, have you?" The big man floundered pitifully.

"Well, fine then," Smallwood said. He held out his hand. "See that you handle Beecher right." He gave Tuckahue's big paw the same stiff, gingerish shake as before and quickly withdrew his hand again.

"Ah won't touch a finger to him," Tuckahue swore fervently. "Ah'll bring him back so you don't even know him."

Smallwood picked up his palette and turned away.

"Well, so long," Tuckahue said heartily. He strode off down the porch.

Smallwood stood before his painting. He was listening to the clump of Tuckahue's brogans. After a moment he heard the car start. The powerful old motor roared and spit and then the auto swung down the drive with its tires humming. Smallwood turned around. He couldn't see Beecher. They must have put him on the floor. He sighed. It was a mess. But what else could he do? And if he said so himself, he had acted honestly. How many other white planters would have apologized to a black man?

He sighed again. The world was hard. It ground down on you like a hard wheel. It made you hard too.

VI

The old motor roared and the tires sang steady on the hard-pan road. No one spoke. Charlie Rentle was busy at the wheel. Harrison Towne sprawled back, chewing the shreds of a dead cigar. Tuckahue had told Harrison about Smallwood's orders but the deputy knew better than to start in on Beecher himself. There were a good many ways of taking a notion out of a niggah and Towne was no fool: his way was always the sheriff's way. The deputy smiled as he thought about it. He hadn't been so bright at school, but politics, by God, was a different matter. He wasn't turnin' out so bad at politics. You just had to know where the fat was — and stay close . . . He lounged back, waiting for his master's voice.

Sheriff Tuckahue was sitting stiffly erect. One long, hairy hand gripped the side of the car; his jaws were locked together and a muscle in his cheek was working. He was frightened! He had been shaken all through by Smallwood's threat to his security — "tired of being sheriff, Mr. Tuckahue?" — Good God, he knew Smallwood! He knew the soft-tongued, friendly way with which Smallwood could finish a man — that upper-class, deadly politeness greasing the cut of the ax: "Sorry, Mr. T., sorry," — as though it were breaking his Goddamned heart. Christ Jesus it was impossible! He'd been sheriff for ten years and now this little barn louse would finish him with a word. Where was the fairness to it? . . . Jesus! — Tuckahue pictured himself chopping cotton again. No, it just wasn't possible. Smallwood *couldn't* play him a card like that. He couldn't be *that* low. Of course he couldn't.

The sheriff relaxed a little. He was beginning to feel easier. The more he thought about it the more ridiculous it obviously became. It was just Smallwood as usual. Smallwood liked to do that — use his power, scare somebody. But still . . . still . . . Rentle! That was it, Rentle! Tuckahue fixed his eyes on the thin back hunched over the wheel. That was the ticket. Get his Gawd damn nephew off the payroll right away. That would stop the tongues from flapping. Even Smallwood had joked about it — yes, the bastard — as if it made any difference to him. And Beecher! Yes. That too! Get Rentle off and bring Beecher back like a stiff shirt that's been through the laundry; bring Beecher back so he dripped honey like the humblest niggah evah lived. By Gawd Smallwood'd have nothin' t'kick about then!

"Hey!" Tuckahue shouted hoarsely at his nephew. "Pull up a minute."

The car stopped. Rentle glanced back over his shoulder. "Ovah to the side! You don't own the road. By Gawd but you're a bonehead!"

Rentle pulled over to the ditch and turned around sharply. He took off his spectacles. "Uncle Sam, you stop talkin' to me like that," he burst out in passionate resentment. "Ah ain't goin' t'stand for it, not a minute more, ah ain't."

Tuckahue snorted.

"You heah me!" Rentle said. "Ah'm tired once an' for all of hearin' your tongue. You speak to me right or ah'm goin' t'quit!"

Tuckahue burst out laughing. "Go ahead," he said. "Ah'm prayin' for it. You turn mah stomach till ah want to vomit. You're makin' a sick man outa me. Go ahead, quit, ah'm waitin'."

"Yes, you are!" Rentle said scornfully.

Tuckahue stopped laughing. He leaned forward. "You quit, didn't you?" he asked softly. "What are you waitin' for?"

For a moment the youth looked at his uncle with a startled expression. Then he put his spectacles back on again. He removed his deputy's badge and undid the cartridge holster with the heavy revolver in it. "All right, Uncle Sam," he said, "you asked for it. Ah'm quittin' right now! But let me tell you somethin': By the time we get into town you're gonna sober up some an' come crawlin' to me. But you ain't gonna get me back so easy. *Ah'm* gonna make the bargain this time!"

Tuckahue's mouth spread wide in a silent, venomous smile. "By the time *we* get into town, Charlie m'boy, *you're* goin' to be still hoofin' the road — that is, unless you can get some fellow niggah t'give you a ride."

"You goin' t'make me walk?" Charlie asked incredulously.

Tuckahue grinned.

Rentle got out of the car. "Uncle Sam," he said, "you're a son of a bitch!" He started off down the road.

"Watch yourself, Charlie," Tuckahue called after him. "Some young buck catch a pretty female like you walkin' alone, he's goin' t'do things to you! You come back all swollen up, your maw ain't gonna like it!"

Deputy Towne let out a loud, wet, laughing snigger. Rentle didn't turn around.

Tuckahue sat bent over. His immense body was shaking with suppressed laughter. He kept slapping a hand on his knee in a gesture of inexpressible amusement.

Towne sniggered lewdly. "You sure told him off, Sam," he said. "You sure told him," he repeated.

"An' ah fired him five minutes ago," Tuckahue burst out suddenly, "only he didn't know it." He bent over again, slapping his knee convulsively. He was helpless with pure joy.

George Beecher, lying on the floor of the car, suddenly raised his head and looked off toward the fields. He had been lying quietly since the car started, with his head pillowed on his arms and with his face turned away from the white men. The racking, convulsive emotion, which had stormed through him in the moment of speaking to Smallwood, was gone. What remained was a feeling of weariness and hunger, and a vague sense of loss as though something had been full in his body but had been drained away. The strange voice within him was quiet now; he only knew that his throat ached and that it pained him to swallow. He didn't think of the future; but he felt it like a faraway pain, like a troubled nerve end buried and waiting in his flesh: the cell, the long days, the white man's court; and the road gang and the nine-pound hammer and the whip, the whip; how many black men come back? He lay quiet wishing he had a drink of water. Then, drifting through the laughter of the white men, came the sound of singing from a church. He raised his head.

When Beecher got to his knees and looked around, Sheriff Tuckahue stopped laughing and eyed him closely. Beecher made him remember Mr. Smallwood. He had almost forgotten about that side of the business. Getting rid of Rentle was only the simplest part. If he wanted to be right with Smallwood again, he had to damn well bring Beecher back turned inside out. And that was as easy as pulling teeth on a mule. The boy had as bad a notion in his eye as any niggah he'd ever seen . . . Tuckahue grunted and cleared his throat. "Where you goin', boy?" he asked with mock humor.

"Just lookin,' boss."

"Aimin' to buy a piece of ground aroun' heah, maybe? Build yourself a house?"

"Nosuh, boss. Church ovah theah. Ah thought maybe ah see someone."

A hundred yards in from the road there was a ramshackle Negro church. One of the door hinges had

broken off and the swelling note of a hymn came clear
through the partly opened doorway. In front of the
church there was a collection of dilapidated Ford cars
and rickety wagons, but there were no people to be
seen.

"Take a long look," Tuckahue said. He winked
at Deputy Towne.

Towne grinned. "Yessir," he said, picking up the
cue, "reckon you ain't nevah goin' t'see that church,
again. You just a poor, unfortunate niggah boy. Ah'm
feelin' right sorry for you."

Beecher lay down in the bottom of the car and
turned his face away. The white men grinned at each
other. Tuckahue reached for his liquor bottle. "Here's
to Avery J. Smallwood," he said. He spit over the side
of the car. Deputy Towne sniggered.

The hot rye gurgled noisily down Tuckahue's
throat. He drained the bottle and flung it into the ditch.
He reached into the side pocket of the car, drew out
another pint and fished for his jackknife.

"You sure put it down," Deputy Towne said
admiringly.

There was no response from the sheriff. He drank
again.

"Heaven's sake," Towne said, "where you put it
all?"

Tuckahue grunted. He bit off a chew of apple
plug and champed down on it hard. Then he exploded
into violent, abusive speech: "Did he offer me a drink?
No, by Gawd, no! Struttin' around on his double heels
—'Ah nevah dirty mah hands on mah own niggahs, Mr.

Tuckahue. That's what ah'm payin' taxes for, Mr. Tuckahue. Ah only drink with gentlemen, Mr. Tuckahue!' — the Gawd damn bantam rooster!"

The sheriff spit violently over the side of the car. He erupted into sudden, unpleasant laughter. "That cow! Ha! Ha! That cow! Ha! Ha! Ha! He's a picture painter, Mr. Towne. He's a friggin' artist. He stands on his front porch painting the ass hole of a cow . . . 'How do you like it, Mr. Tuckahue?' he asks me. 'Fine,' ah says, 'real as life, Mr. Smallwood . . .'" The sheriff shook with venomous, drunken laughter. "Gawd Almighty, Mr. Towne, that cow looked more like the hind end of a trolley car than anything ah evah seen. Put four wheels under it and it'd roll right off down the veranda."

Deputy Towne joined half-heartedly in the sheriff's laughter. He was worried by the presence of Beecher. Beecher might report back to Smallwood. He winked at Tuckahue and jerked his thumb, but the sheriff waved his hand deprecatingly and gulped some more rye. His head was rolling around now. The new bottle was half-empty. Land sakes, Towne reflected, the old buzzard's getting sure shot this time. Never saw him take so much in one stand before.

"The Smallwoods!" Tuckahue burst out suddenly. "Oh the blue-blooded, blue-balled Smallwoods. '*We* are the old South. *We* are the aristocrats. There's gentlemen's blood in us' — an' niggah blood too," he added snarling.

Towne sniggered.

" 'We don't do our own dirty work,' " Tuckahue continued. " 'Oh no! We keep our hands clean. There's French per*fume* on us. We don't even wipe ourselves. Oh no. We *pay* for that!' "

"Hey!" Towne jerked his thumb toward Beecher. "Take it easy, will you?" he whispered.

"Aaaah ! He won't talk!" Tuckahue dug his knuckles into Beecher's back in a gesture of drunken affection. "He won't talk. You like Smallwood less'n ah do, don't you, dark boy? Sure you do!" He thumped Beecher on the back with the knuckles of his closed fist. "Sure you do," he repeated.

Beecher, lying on his stomach with his head pillowed on his arms, felt Tuckahue's fist like a faraway pound on his back. It was only half-felt, vague, like a stray moth troubling his face at night. He was not aware of what the white men were saying. He had been lying in a doze with the hot sun comforting his body. His body seemed to suck up the sun, drinking it in to fill that hollowness inside. And his thoughts had drifted back to the noon hour in the fields, when his mother would come out with some black-eyed peas and a piece of cornbread, and he would stop for a moment to eat, and there would be a little breeze stirring the dead air. The white men's talk was a buzz in his ears and he listened through their jawing for the sweet song from the church which rose and fell, and swung him up on a deep swell, and then died down again. It comforted him like the warm hand of a brush fire filling their room in winter, or like the deep, warm goodness of his mother when the mule kicked him and he had been sick with fever and she had pressed him soft to her breast.

Then he felt a hand tugging at his shoulder, and he heard the sheriff talking to him. "Turn around, boy, ah want t'look at you."

Beecher turned his face to the white men.

Tuckahue was examining him with reddened, bloodshot eyes. "Pshaw — you're a nice lookin' dark boy," he said. "What you want t'go gettin' yourself notions for?"

Beecher didn't reply.

Tuckahue's face became crafty. He leaned forward. "Listen, boy," he offered confidentially, "that Smallwood snake told me t'take you down to jail an' beat the hell out of you. But ah ain't goin' t'do that, boy. Ah'm your friend . . . You heah me?"

The singing died out of Beecher's ears. The car came back; and the white deputies; and the nine-pound hammer, the jail and the whip. He heard the sheriff say it again: "Ah'm your friend, boy." And the deep, strange whisper inside of him began again: "No friend; he no friend; white sheriff no friend." Beecher raised his head. "Yessuh, boss," he said with familiar, practiced humility, "thank you, boss."

"But you got a notion in your eye and that's bad," the sheriff said. "Bad for a niggah boy to have a notion in his eye."

"Say, Sam, how about movin' from heah?" Towne asked. "It's *hot*."

Tuckahue wagged a solemn, bony finger at Beecher. "You got a notion in your eye, boy."

"No, ah ain't, Cap'n," Beecher said humbly.

"Ah say you have!" The contradiction was stern. "Don't you talk back to me, George."

"Listen, Sam," Towne said, "for Heaven's sakes — it's *hot*. Let's get goin'."

"George," Tuckahue said, "why'd you hit a white man?"

Beecher was silent.

"Hey!" Tuckahue prodded him with his foot. "When ah put you a question, you better answer."

Beecher sat up slowly. "You know why ah hit him, boss."

"Well!" Tuckahue looked Beecher over with rising anger. "You're a sassy, little bastard, ain't you? . . . Regular Smallwood niggah. Yessir! Always tell a Smallwood niggah by his sassy tongue."

Deputy Towne hitched his belt and leaned forward. "Why'd you slug Ed Bailey? Was that yallah girl yours?"

"She warn't nobody's girl," Beecher replied sullenly. "She was just a little chile."

"What's the mattah?" Tuckahue laughed. "You want 'em to consent? Bailey don't want 'em to consent. Nossir, he don't like 'em to consent!"

Towne sniggered.

Beecher lay down suddenly and turned his face away from the white men. Tuckahue stopped laughing. He reached down slowly and grabbed Beecher by the strap of his overalls. He pulled him up to a sitting position.

The Negro youth and the white man stared at each other.

"Beecher," Tuckahue said softly, "ah-don't-like-you. You're a Smallwood niggah! You got notions! Ah reckon ah'm gonna have t'learn you somethin'. Ah'm gonna have t'learn you how to *crawl,* Beecher."

The slow, hot whisper began inside Beecher, the stubborn tide pulsed and swelled and rose up in his throat. "Ah'm tired of crawlin', white boss," he said. "Ah ain't gone t'crawl for nobody no more."

Tuckahue stared at him. His little, flinty eyes were gleaming. "Beecher," he said softly, "ah'm goin' t'teach you what this heah world's like you're livin' in! Ah'm goin' t'teach you the way of things. *Everybody* crawls, Beecher. Ah crawl for Mr. Smallwood, Deputy Towne crawls for me, an' every niggah crawls for every white man. That's how it's gotta be!"

The Negro youth wet his lips. "Ah don't crawl no more," he said. "Ah got mah bellyfull!"

"Deputy Towne," Tuckahue said softly, without taking his eyes from Beecher's face, "get in the front an' start drivin'."

Towne stepped over the seat and started the car. The sheriff opened his hand slowly, releasing Beecher, who sank down to the floor. Tuckahue took another drink and corked the bottle. He was still staring at Beecher with bloodshot, gleaming eyes.

Beecher lay with his head pillowed on his arms. His face was turned away from the sheriff. The car jerked forward. The singing receded until he could no longer hear it. "Ah don't keer," the voice whispered inside of him. "Don't keer. Don't keer."

Sheriff Tuckahue lay back in the car. His head was swimming from the whiskey. He knew he had had too much but he felt better for it. He felt fine. He felt full and free inside, strong and swollen like a running river, flowing and roaring inside. He felt like seeing Smallwood now. Put one hand on the back of his neck and squeeze just a little. Dig his fingers in! Gawd, he felt fine. He'd like to see that woman again. Christ Jesus, that big, bouncing, lovely bitch. She'd remember all right. She wouldn't forget him in a hurry. Put a hand on her where she was soft and juicy and make her yell just once. Make her yell. She wouldn't forget him that time. Tuckahue gripped the side of the car. He wanted a good niggah, did he? Smallwood was boss, wasn't he? And he wanted a good niggah, didn't he? All right! Before Tuckahue was through that niggah'd be crawlin' on his hands and knees. He'd kiss the floor in front of every white man he saw. Mean bastard! Stubborn as a mule! Head full of ideas! Had a belly-full, hey? By Gawd a fine how do you do. Regular Smallwood niggah. All right, he'd iron him out. And nevah touch a hand to him. Nevah put a finger to him! Tuckahue suddenly burst out laughing. He smashed his hand down hard on the upholstery. His mouth opened wide and his thin lips puckered back from the big, horse teeth. "Harrison," he yelled, "Harrison, Gawd damn you, stop at Shaney's when we get there! Ah want to buy me a bottle!"

"Say listen, you got some left, ain't you?" Towne called back. "Wait'll we come home."

Tuckahue laughed. "Stop at Shaney's, Gawd damn you, Harrison," he said.

"Okay!" The deputy assented, and swore exasperatedly to himself.

The sheriff leaned back. He looked at the quiet body of the black boy and his eyes glittered with pleasure. He felt marvelous. He felt like jumping up and yelling out loud. He wished he could see Smallwood now.

They came to a four corners where there was a gas station and a general store. Tuckahue lurched out of the car, winked broadly at Deputy Towne and strode inside. Towne knitted his brows and wondered what the hell the damn fool was up to. In another minute Tuckahue came back. He ran down the steps of the store talking excitedly to Shaney, the storekeeper, a bald, fat, little man of forty with a snub-nosed, monkey face.

"By Christ," Tuckahue shouted, winking at Towne, "we gotta run for it! There's a lynch party comin' after George!"

Beecher jerked up violently into a sitting position. He stared at the white men with sudden, bitter fear in his eyes.

"Yessir," Shaney said, "I just got a phone call. Ed Bailey's friends are out after the niggah who beat him up. Is that him?" he asked, pointing. "Man, you're outa luck! Ah wouldn't change necks with you!" Shaney clapped his hand over his mouth to stifle his laughter.

Towne caught wise and his face split into an amused grin.

Beecher drew a deep, painful breath. "You gone t'let them take me, boss?"

"Hell, no!" Tuckahue said bombastically. He slammed his fist down on the upholstery in a melodramatic gesture. "They catch up with us, ah'm gone t'defend you!"

"You bettah hide him," Shaney said. "Ah'll get you somethin'." He ran off behind the store.

"Is your gun loaded?" Tuckahue demanded excitedly of Deputy Towne. "Keep it on the seat! Keep it handy!"

Towne flipped his gun barrel ostentatiously. "Ah'll protect you with mah life, niggah boy!"

Shaney came running around the side of the store dragging a maggoty, old, mule blanket behind him. "Cover him with this," he said. "It stinks a little but it'll hide him."

Tuckahue pushed Beecher down and flung the blanket over him. The white men shook with silent laughter. The sheriff leaped into the back seat. "Give it all it's got, Mr. Towne," he ordered melodramatically.

"Stop at Benny Wilkerson's," Shaney advised. "Ah'll phone him when the mob passes heah."

"Right!" The car shot forward. Shaney stood in the middle of the road shaking with helpless laughter. Then he caught hold of himself and ran into the store to telephone his friends.

Beecher lay under the stinking mule blanket, suck-

ing violently, painfully, for air, with his mouth gaping
open. His fists were clenched and his cramped body
felt twisted into a thousand coils which snaked and
writhed inside of him, begging to break loose, to snap
out, to run free. The swaying, roaring, bouncing car
kept hammering him cruelly on his knees, his elbows,
his hip bones. His head seemed on fire with sudden
pains, there was an unendurable buzzing in his ears
and his mind kept hammering the same thing over and
over again like a wireless beating out a signal: "Whut
they gonna do? Whut they gonna do? Whut they gonna
do?" Then, deep inside, the voice began to whisper;
it spoke to him coldly, cruelly, without pity: "They
ain't gone help you. White boss don't help you. Turn
you over. Done now. You done, George." Beecher listened, and his whole being wept in frenzy at what he
heard. "They running!" he pleaded with the voice.
"They not waiting! They ain't gonna turn me ovah!"
But the low voice whispered again its cold, final warning and again he thrust it aside, clinging bitterly, hysterically, to his shred of hope.

Then he heard the white man's voice close to his
ear. Tuckahue had leaned forward and raised the
blanket. The voice was warm with comfort but Tuckahue's face was sly and wrinkled with glee as he looked
down at the boy. Beecher was scared all right. The
niggah boy was scaring plenty. By Gawd Tuckahue
was goin' t'bring back a sharecropper like Smallwood
never saw before. He'd bring him back dripping honey
like he was a comb of beeswax and he'd say, "Heah

you are, Mr. Smallwood, how do you like that? Ah done just what you told me, Mr. Smallwood."

"Don't be scared, boy," Tuckahue said in a soft, sly, exultant tone, "you'll be protected! They ain't gone lynch you! Nossir! They said they was goin' t' cut off the hand that struck Ed Bailey — burn it before your eyes they said — but they ain't gonna do it, nossir! Ah'll protect you, boy."

Tuckahue dropped the blanket back over Beecher's head. His upper lip puckered in silent laughter. He pulled out the bottle of liquor and finished off what was left. He flung it over the side. The car raced madly through the countryside.

Beecher lay on the floor sobbing from helplessness. He didn't know what to believe. There was nothing to believe. There was nothing to do. If he could fight. If he could run somewhere. If he could do something . . . The sheriff's voice came to him again. "Don't be afraid, boy, you don't need to be afraid."

"Ah ain't afraid," Beecher burst out in a wild cry, "but ah cain't lay *heah*. Ah can't just wait *heah*."

"Sure you can, you got to," Tuckahue said. "Think of something, boy! Don't think of the lynchin'! They ain't gonna get you. They said they was goin' t'tie you to the back of a car — drag you till you scraped to death — but they ain't agonna do that, boy. Think of something! Think of your mammy. She loves you, doesn't she? She wouldn't want anything to happen to you? Think of some nice, juicy, yellah gal, boy. You got a wife?"

"Lord Jesus doan' talk like that," Beecher cried. "Let me go! Let me get out of heah! Let me run for it!" He pushed up on the floor. "Ah take ma chance, white boss! Let me run!"

"You're crazy, boy," Tuckahue told him gleefully. "You get caught sure that way." He pushed him down on the floor again. Beecher fell back, his body quivering frantically. The voice kept beating like a drum inside — "white man turn you ovah, George — turn you ovah, George, . . . " and he crushed it down, stamped on it, trying with his whole soul to believe the white man was true.

"We'll get you through," Tuckahue said sweetly, comfortingly. "You just put your mind on some nice yallah girl. Tell yourself she's got no clothes on; make believe you're doin' things to her, makin' her yell, squeezin' her where she's soft. Those ridin' bosses said you ain't nevah gonna have a woman again, George. But don't you believe 'em. They said they was gonna cut off that black thing of yours an' give it to Ed Bailey to wear on his watch chain — but they'll nevah do it, George." Tuckahue's face became exultant. "You heah me, George," he shouted, "they ain't gonna lynch you. They ain't gonna stick their jack knives into you. Ah ain't gonna let them burn *you,* George. Oh no! Ha! Certainly not, George. Ha! Ha! Ha! You just stay heah, George."

And then Beecher knew. He knew now. They weren't going to protect him. They were going to hand him over. God! Oh Jesus God! A cry of infinite horror convulsed his whole body. It slashed through him inside — through his heart and lungs and belly, crying "God. Oh Jesus God!" . . . And then it was over. For one moment he drank down the fullest measure of horror and fear that he had ever known, and then it was over. It passed away. He was left free of it. And in its place there was something else. He felt it flaming up, burning and swelling in his body — hatred, pure burning hatred, and contempt — and over everything, like a cloth of silk on his soul, a sense of pride, of unutterable dignity and pride. He would die now, he knew it, but he was not afraid! He had said his say to Smallwood, he had struck his blow at Bailey, he would not be afraid now! Yes, sweet Jesus, he had spoken out! One black man had spoken out! They wouldn't see him afraid now!

Beecher lay quiet. He felt strangely, marvelously calm. He felt like a deep river rolling down hill. The roaring of the waterfall was strong in his ears, but the silk, the deep silk was folding him close.

Then Sheriff Tuckahue screamed aloud in mock fear: "Step on it, Harry, there's cars behind us." Deputy Towne let out a howl and drove the car forward. They were burning up the road at seventy an hour. "Christ Jesus, there's *six* cars behind us," Tuckahue cried. "Loaded up with men an' guns! Comin' after us!"

"Are they gainin'?" Towne laughed.

"Ah can't tell! . . . No, we're beatin' 'em! They ain't catchin' us," Tuckahue cried in mock triumph. "Keep your head down, George, we'll save you — Hey!" The sheriff caught his breath. "We're trapped!" He pointed ahead at the empty road. "There's six more cars up ahead! They got us, Harry. We'll have to hand poor George ovah. They're gonna lynch poor George. Slow down, Harry! They're blocking the road!"

Towne cut his gas. The car began to lose speed.

And then the wave of pride and dignity caught George Beecher and lifted him high. His heart was on fire with wild singing and defiance. Not for him! No rope for him! Never, never, never for him!

And in one violent movement Beecher leaped to his feet; and then fiercely, proudly, he flung himself over the side of the car.

VII

When Avery Smallwood put down his telephone, he stood like a man transfixed. He felt nauseous with horror. It was a terrible thing. It was simply incredible. And somehow he felt guilty. It was as though he were responsible for the death of that boy. But it wasn't true. He knew it wasn't.

His wife came into the room and he told her, falteringly, what had happened. The tears came into her eyes and her pretty face twisted with shock and pity. He wanted to comfort her but he couldn't find anything to say. What on earth had made the boy do a thing like that anyway? Just a crazy notion about escaping. But so foolish, so damn foolish. And how could you foresee it? You couldn't know in advance about a thing like that. And he had had to do something in order to teach the boy.

"Oh Christ! . . ." Smallwood swore aloud. He sat down and gripped his head with both hands. What a hard world it was. What a bitter, miserable place. Poor Beecher lying on the road with his head crushed. A man just had to make himself hard, and then try to forget about it.

Smallwood got up. He went to the sideboard and poured himself a drink. He knew what would happen to him now: He would drift into one of his periods of depression. So damn confusing this life was. And now he wouldn't be able to go back to his painting till the middle of the week, or even later. It was hard. A man had to be hard to take things the way they were.

He got up and went out to the veranda. He didn't know what to do with himself. He hadn't felt so upset in ages. It was simply shocking . . . For want of something better, Smallwood started cleaning his paint-brushes.

The Happiest
Man
on Earth

The Happiest Man on Earth

Jesse felt ready to weep. He had been sitting in the shanty waiting for Tom to appear, grateful for the chance to rest his injured foot, quietly, joyously anticipating the moment when Tom would say, "Why, of course, Jesse, you can start whenever you're ready!"

For two weeks he had been pushing himself, from Kansas City, Missouri, to Tulsa, Oklahoma, through nights of rain and a week of scorching sun, without sleep or a decent meal, sustained by the vision of that

---

"The Happiest Man on Earth" was first published in 1938.

one moment. And then Tom had come into the office. He had come in quickly, holding a sheaf of papers in his hand; he had glanced at Jesse only casually, it was true — but long enough. He had not known him. He had turned away . . . And Tom Brackett was his brother-in-law.

Was it his clothes? Jesse knew he looked terrible. He had tried to spruce up at a drinking fountain in the park, but even that had gone badly; in his excitement he had cut himself shaving, an ugly gash down the side of his cheek. And nothing could get the red gumbo dust out of his suit even though he had slapped himself till both arms were worn out . . . Or was it just that he had changed so much?

True, they hadn't seen each other for five years; but Tom looked five years older, that was all. He was still Tom. God! Was he so different?

Brackett finished his telephone call. He leaned back in his swivel chair and glanced over at Jesse with small, clear, blue eyes that were suspicious and unfriendly. He was a heavy, paunchy man of forty-five, auburn-haired, rather dour-looking; his face was meaty, his features pronounced and forceful, his nose somewhat bulbous and reddish-hued at the tip. He looked like a solid, decent, capable businessman who was commander of his local branch of the American Legion — which he was. He surveyed Jesse with cold indifference, manifestly unwilling to spend time on him. Even the way he chewed his toothpick seemed contemptuous to Jesse.

"Yes?" Brackett said suddenly. "What do you want?"

His voice was decent enough, Jesse admitted. He had expected it to be worse. He moved up to the wooden counter that partitioned the shanty. He thrust a hand nervously through his tangled hair.

"I guess you don't recognize me, Tom," he said falteringly. "I'm Jesse Fulton."

"Huh?" Brackett said. That was all.

"Yes, I am, and Ella sends you her love."

Brackett rose and walked over to the counter until they were face to face. He surveyed Fulton incredulously, trying to measure the resemblance to his brother-in-law as he remembered him. This man was tall, about thirty. That fitted! He had straight good features and a lank erect body. That was right too. But the face was too gaunt, the body too spiny under the baggy clothes for him to be sure. His brother-in-law had been a solid, strong, young man with muscle and beef to him. It was like looking at a faded, badly taken photograph and trying to recognize the subject: The resemblance was there but the difference was tremendous. He searched the eyes. They at least seemed definitely familiar, gray, with a curiously shy but decent look in them. He had liked that about Fulton.

Jesse stood quiet. Inside he was seething. Brackett was like a man examining a piece of broken-down horseflesh; there was a look of pure pity in his eyes. It made Jesse furious. He knew he wasn't as far gone as all that.

"Yes, I believe you are," Bracket said finally, "but you sure have changed."

"By God, it's five years, ain't it?" Jesse said resentfully. "You only saw me a couple of times anyway." Then, to himself, with his lips locked together, in mingled vehemence and shame, "What if I have changed? Don't everybody? I ain't no corpse."

"You was solid looking," Brackett continued softly, in the same tone of incredulous wonder. "You lost weight, I guess?"

Jesse kept silent. He needed Brackett too much to risk antagonizing him. But it was only by deliberate effort that he could keep from boiling over. The pause lengthened, became painful. Brackett flushed. "Jiminy Christmas, excuse me," he burst out in apology. He jerked the counter up. "Come in. Take a seat. Good God, boy" — he grasped Jesse's hand and shook it — "I am glad to see you; don't think anything else! You just looked so peaked."

"It's all right," Jesse murmured. He sat down, thrusting his hand through his curly, tangled hair.

"Why are you limping?"

"I stepped on a stone; it jagged a hole through my shoe." Jesse pulled his feet back under the chair. He was ashamed of his shoes. They had come from the relief originally, and two weeks on the road had about finished them. All morning, with a kind of delicious, foolish solemnity, he had been vowing to himself that before anything else, before even a suit of clothes, he was going to buy himself a brand-new strong pair of shoes.

Brackett kept his eyes off Jesse's feet. He knew what was bothering the boy and it filled his heart with pity. The whole thing was appalling. He had never seen anyone who looked more down-and-out. His sister had been writing to him every week, but she hadn't told him they were as badly-off as this.

"Well now, listen," Brackett began, "tell me things. How's Ella?"

"Oh, she's pretty good," Jesse replied absently. He had a soft, pleasing, rather shy voice that went with his soft gray eyes. He was worrying over how to get started.

"And the kids?"

"Oh, they're fine . . . Well, you know," Jesse added, becoming more attentive, "the young one has to wear a brace. He can't run around, you know. But he's smart. He draws pictures and he does things, you know."

"Yes," Brackett said. "That's good." He hesitated. There was a moment's silence. Jesse fidgeted in his chair. Now that the time had arrived, he felt awkward. Brackett leaned forward and put his hand on Jesse's knee. "Ella didn't tell me things were so bad for you, Jesse. I might have helped."

"Well, goodness," Jesse returned softly, "you been having your own troubles, ain't you?"

"Yes." Brackett leaned back. His ruddy face became mournful and darkly bitter. "You know I lost my hardware shop?"

"Well sure, of course," Jesse answered, surprised. "You wrote us. That's what I mean."

"I forgot," Brackett said. "I keep on being surprised over it myself. Not that it was worth much," he
added bitterly. "It was running downhill for three
years. I guess I just wanted it because it was mine."
He laughed pointlessly, without mirth. "Well, tell me
about yourself," he asked. "What happened to the
job you had?"

Jesse burst out abruptly, with agitation, "Let it
wait, Tom, I got something on my mind."

"It ain't you and Ella?" Brackett interrupted
anxiously.

"Why no!" Jesse sat back. "Why, however did
you come to think that? Why Ella and me . . . " He
stopped, laughing. "Why, Tom, I'm just crazy about
Ella. Why she's just wonderful. She's just my whole
life, Tom."

"Excuse me. Forget it." Brackett chuckled uncomfortably, turned away. The naked intensity of the
youth's burst of love had upset him. It made him wish
savagely that he could do something for them. They
were too decent to have had it so hard. Ella was like
this boy too, shy and a little soft.

"Tom, listen," Jesse said, "I come here on pur-
pose." He thrust his hand through his hair. "I want
you to help me."

"Damn it, boy," Brackett groaned. He had been
expecting this. "I can't much. I only get thirty-five a
week and I'm damn grateful for it."

"Sure, I know," Jesse emphasized excitedly. He
was feeling once again the wild, delicious agitation
that had possessed him in the early hours of the morn-

ing. "I know you can't help us with money! But we met a man who works for you! He was in our city! He said you could give me a job!"

"Who said?"

"Oh, why didn't you tell me?" Jesse burst out reproachfully. "Why, as soon as I heard of it I started out. For two weeks now I been pushing ahead like crazy."

Brackett groaned aloud. "You come walking from Kansas City in two weeks so I could give you a job?"

"Sure, Tom, of course. What else could I do?"

"God Almighty, there ain't no jobs, Jesse! It's a slack season. And you don't know this oil business. It's special. I got my Legion friends here, but they couldn't do nothing now. Don't you think I'd ask for you as soon as there was a chance?"

Jesse felt stunned. The hope of the last two weeks seemed rolling up into a ball of agony in his stomach. Then, frantically, he cried, "But listen, this man said *you* could hire! He told me! He drives trucks for you! He said you always need men!"

"Oh! . . . You mean my department?" Brackett said in a low voice.

"Yes, Tom. That's it!"

"Oh no, you don't want to work in my department," Brackett told him in the same low voice. "You don't know what it is."

"Yes, I do," Jesse insisted. "He told me all about it, Tom. You're a dispatcher, ain't you? You send the dynamite trucks out?"

"Who was the man, Jesse?"

"Everett, Everett, I think."

"Egbert? Man about my size?" Brackett asked slowly.

"Yes, Egbert. He wasn't a phony, was he?"

Brackett laughed. For the second time his laughter was curiously without mirth. "No, he wasn't a phony." Then, in a changed voice: "Jiminy, boy, you should have asked me before you trekked all the way down here."

"Oh, I didn't want to," Jesse explained with naive cunning. "I knew you'd say no. He told me it was risky work, Tom. But I don't care."

Brackett locked his fingers together. His solid, meaty face became very hard. "I'm going to say no anyway, Jesse."

Jesse cried out. It had not occurred to him that Brackett would not agree. It had seemed as though reaching Tulsa were the only problem he had to face. "Oh no," he begged, "you can't. Ain't there any jobs, Tom?"

"Sure there's jobs. There's even Egbert's job if you want it."

"He's quit?"

"He's dead!"

"Oh!"

"On the job, Jesse. Last night if you want to know."

"Oh!" . . . Then, "I don't care!"

"Now you listen to me," Brackett said. "I'll tell you a few things that you should have asked before you started out. It ain't dynamite you drive. They don't use anything as safe as dynamite in drilling oil wells. They wish they could, but they can't. It's nitroglycerin! Soup!"

"But I know," Jesse told him reassuringly. "He advised me, Tom. You don't have to think I don't know."

"Shut up a minute," Brackett ordered angrily. "Listen! You just have to look at this soup, see? You just cough loud and it blows! You know how they transport it? In a can that's shaped like this, see, like a fan? That's to give room for compartments, because each compartment has to be lined with rubber. That's the only way you can even think of handling it."

"Listen, Tom . . ."

"Now wait a minute, Jesse. For God's sake just put your mind to this. I know you had your heart set on a job, but you've got to understand. This stuff goes only in special trucks! At night! They got to follow a special route! They can't go through any city! If they lay over, it's got to be in a special garage! Don't you see what that means? Don't that tell you how dangerous it is?"

"I'll drive careful," Jesse said. "I know how to handle a truck. I'll drive slow."

Brackett groaned. "Do you think Egbert didn't drive careful or know how to handle a truck?"

"Tom," Jesse said earnestly, "you can't scare me. I got my mind fixed on only one thing: Egbert said he was getting a dollar a mile. He was making five to six hundred dollars a month for half a month's work, he said. Can I get the same?"

"Sure you can get the same," Brackett told him

savagely. "A dollar a mile. It's easy. But why do you think the company has to pay so much? It's easy — until you run over a stone that your headlights didn't pick out, like Egbert did. Or get a blowout! Or get something in your eye so the wheel twists and you jar the truck! Or any other God damn thing that nobody ever knows! We can't ask Egbert what happened to him. There's no truck to give any evidence. There's no corpse. There's nothing! Maybe tomorrow somebody'll find a piece of twisted steel way off in a cornfield. But we never find the driver. Not even a fingernail. All we know is that he don't come in on schedule. Then we wait for the police to call us. You know what happened last night? Something went wrong on a bridge. Maybe Egbert was nervous. Maybe he brushed the side with his fender. Only there's no bridge anymore. No truck. No Egbert. Do you understand now? That's what you get for your God damn dollar a mile!"

There was a moment of silence. Jesse sat twisting his long thin hands. His mouth was sagging open, his face was agonized. Then he shut his eyes and spoke softly. "I don't care about that, Tom. You told me. Now you got to be good to me and give me the job."

Brackett slapped the palm of his hand down on his desk. "No!"

"Listen, Tom," Jesse said softly, "you just don't understand." He opened his eyes. They were filled with tears. They made Brackett turn away. "Just look at me, Tom. Don't that tell you enough? What did you think of me when you first saw me? You thought: 'Why don't that bum go away and stop panhandling?' Didn't you,

Tom? Tom, I just can't live like this any more. I got to
be able to walk down the street with my head up."

"You're crazy," Brackett muttered. "Every year
there's one out of five drivers gets killed. That's the
average. What's worth that?"

"Is my life worth anything now? We're just starvin'
at home, Tom. They ain't put us back on relief yet."

"Then you should have told me," Brackett exclaimed harshly. "It's your own damn fault. A man has
no right to have false pride when his family ain't eating.
I'll borrow some money and we'll telegraph it to Ella.
Then you go home and get back on relief."

"And then what?"

"And then wait, God damn it! You're no old man.
You got no right to throw your life away. Sometime
you'll get a job."

"No!" Jesse jumped up. "No. I believed that too.
But I don't now," he cried passionately. "I ain't getting
a job no more than you're getting your hardware store
back. I lost my skill, Tom. Linotyping is skilled work.
I'm rusty now. I've been six years on relief. The only
work I've had is pick and shovel. When I got that job
this spring, I was supposed to be an A-1 man. But I
wasn't. And they got new machines now. As soon as the
slack started, they let me out."

"So what?" Brackett said harshly. "Ain't there
others jobs?"

"How do I know?" Jesse replied. "There ain't been
one for six years. I'd even be afraid to take one now.
It's been too hard waiting so many weeks to get back
on relief."

"Well, you got to have some courage," Brackett shouted. "You've got to keep up hope."

"I got all the courage you want," Jesse retorted vehemently, "but no, I ain't got no hope. The hope has dried up in me in six years waiting. You're the only hope I got."

"You're crazy," Brackett muttered. "I won't do it. For God's sake think of Ella for a minute."

"Don't you know I'm thinking about her?" Jesse asked softly. He plucked at Brackett's sleeve. "That's what decided me, Tom." His voice became muted into a hushed, pained, whisper. "The night Egbert was at our house I looked at Ella like I'd seen her for the first time. She ain't pretty anymore, Tom!" Brackett jerked his head and moved away. Jesse followed him, taking a deep, sobbing breath. "Don't that tell you, Tom? Ella was like a little doll or something, you remember. I couldn't walk down the street without somebody turning to look at her. She ain't twenty-nine yet, Tom, and she ain't pretty no more."

Brackett sat down with his shoulders hunched up wearily. He gripped his hands together and sat leaning forward, staring at the floor.

Jesse stood over him, his gaunt face flushed with emotion, almost unpleasant in its look of pleading and bitter humility. "I ain't done right for Ella, Tom. Ella deserved better. This is the only chance I see in my whole life to do something for her. I've just been a failure."

"Don't talk nonsense," Brackett commented without rancor. You ain't a failure. No more than me.

There's millions of men in the identical situation. It's just the depression, or the recession, or the God damn New Deal, or . . . !" He swore and lapsed into silence.

"Oh no," Jesse corrected him in a knowing, sorrowful tone, "those things maybe excuse other men. But not me. It was up to me to do better. This is my own fault!"

"Oh, beans!" Brackett said. "It's more sun spots than it's you!"

Jesse's face turned an unhealthy mottled red. It looked swollen. "Well I don't care," he cried wildly. "I don't care! You got to give me this! I got to lift my head up. I went through one stretch of hell, but I can't go through another. You want me to keep looking at my little boy's legs and tell myself if I had a job he wouldn't be like that? Every time he walks he says to me, 'I got soft bones from the rickets and you give it to me because you didn't feed me right.' Jesus Christ, Tom, you think I'm going to sit there and watch him like that another six years?"

Brackett leaped to his feet. "So what if you do?" he shouted. "You say you're thinking about Ella. How's she going to like it when you get killed?"

"Maybe I won't," Jesse pleaded. "I've got to have some luck sometime."

"That's what they all think," Brackett replied scornfully. "When you take this job, your luck is a question mark. The only thing certain is that sooner or later you get killed."

"Okay then," Jesse shouted back. "Then I do! But meanwhile I got something, don't I? I can buy a pair of shoes. Look at me! I can buy a suit that don't say 'Relief' by the way it fits. I can smoke cigarettes. I can buy some candy for the kids. I can eat some myself. Yes, by God, I want to eat some candy. I want a glass of beer once a day. I want Ella dressed up. I want her to eat meat three times a week, four times maybe. I want to take my family to the movies."

Brackett sat down. "Oh, shut up," he said wearily.

"No," Jesse told him softly, passionately, "you can't get rid of me. Listen, Tom," he pleaded, "I got it all figured out. On six hundred a month look how much I can save! If I last only three months, look how much it is . . . a thousand dollars . . . more! And maybe I'll last longer. Maybe a couple years. I can fix Ella up for life!"

"You said it," Brackett interposed. "I suppose you think she'll enjoy living when you're on a job like that?"

"I got it all figured out," Jesse answered excitedly. "She don't know, see? I tell her I make only forty. You put the rest in a bank account for her, Tom."

"Oh, shut up," Brackett said. "You think you'll be happy? Every minute, waking and sleeping, you'll be wondering if tomorrow you'll be dead. And the worst days will be your days off, when you're not driving. They have to give you every other day free to get your nerve back. And you lay around the house eating your heart out. That's how happy you'll be."

Jesse laughed. "I'll be happy! Don't you worry, I'll be so happy, I'll be singing. Lord God, Tom, I'm going to feel proud of myself for the first time in seven years!"

"Oh, shut up, shut up," Brackett said.

The little shanty became silent. After a moment Jesse whispered: "You got to, Tom. You got to. You got to."

Again there was silence. Brackett raised both hands to his head, pressing the palms against his temples.

"Tom, Tom . . ." Jesse said.

Brackett sighed. "Oh, God damn it," he said finally, "all right, I'll take you on, God help me." His voice was low, hoarse, infinitely weary. "If you're ready to drive tonight, you can drive tonight."

Jesse didn't answer. He couldn't. Brackett looked up. The tears were running down Jesse's face. He was swallowing and trying to speak, but only making an absurd, gasping noise.

"I'll send a wire to Ella," Brackett said in the same hoarse, weary voice. "I'll tell her you got a job, and you'll send her fare in a couple of days. You'll have some money then — that is, if you last the week out, you jackass!"

Jesse only nodded. His heart felt so close to bursting that he pressed both hands against it, as though to hold it locked within his breast.

"Come back here at six o'clock," Brackett said. "Here's some money. Eat a good meal."

"Thanks," Jesse whispered.

"Wait a minute," Brackett said. "Here's my address." He wrote it on a piece of paper, "Take any car going that way. Ask the conductor where to get off. Take a bath and get some sleep."

"Thanks," Jesse said. "Thanks, Tom."

"Oh, get out of here," Brackett said.

"Tom."

"What?"

"I just . . ." Jesse stopped. Brackett saw his face. The eyes were still glistening with tears, but the gaunt face was shining now with a kind of fierce radiance.

Brackett turned away. "I'm busy," he said.

Jesse went out. The wet film blinded him, but the whole world seemed to have turned golden. He limped slowly, with the blood pounding his temples and a wild, incommunicable joy in his heart. "I'm the happiest man in the world," he whispered to himself. "I'm the happiest man on the whole earth."

Brackett sat watching till finally Jesse turned the corner of the alley and disappeared. Then he hunched himself over with his head in his hands. His heart was beating painfully like something old and clogged. He listened to it as it beat. He sat in desperate tranquillity, gripping his head in his hands.

Sunday
Morning
on
Twentieth Street

Sunday Morning on Twentieth Street

It was a fine day in early Spring. Bright sunshine flooded the street where a group of boys in Sunday clothes were playing ball. In most of the tenements the windows were up. Clean-shaven men in collarless shirts

"Sunday Morning on Twentieth Street" was first published in 1940.

or in underwear, women with aprons or sloppy pink wrappers leaned on the sills and gazed with aimless interest at the street, the sky, those who were passing below. Thus they would spend most of every Sunday morning through the coming summer and now, in the first flush of mild weather, they had already taken up their posts. The street rang with the animated bickerings of the boys at their game, with the click of a girl's shoes as she skipped rope, with the muted sounds of a dozen unseen radios.

Into this familiar scene came a sudden intruder: an odd-looking ambulance with glazed windows. It turned into the street quietly, moved along slowly as the driver searched for a number, and then came to a stop before a rooming house — a drab, four-story building of yellowish, soot-stained brick. In the tenement windows above all eyes turned to the ambulance. On the street all games stopped and, in an instant, the ambulance was surrounded by children.

Those who knew why it had come told the others. An hour earlier there had been a police car and, still earlier, two men from the gas company. The odor of gas emanating from the building had been so strong that it had made church-goers sniff as they passed by on the street.

The youngsters who clustered around the ambulance ranged from four to fourteen. Most of them were of Irish stock, the children of longshoremen and truck-drivers, of subway workers and laborers. The boys were wearing their once-a-week suits, the girls had on de-

corous, homemade dresses. Only one little Italian lad
had on stained, blue denim trousers as though it were
any old day of the week. A few of the youngest children
had begun giggling with excitement when the ambulance appeared, but most of the others had become
rather quiet. They stood watching, neither shocked nor
amused, their faces knowing and adult grave. Yet, as
the two drab men in the front seat of the ambulance
stepped out and walked toward the door of the rooming house, the boys followed them with quiet, compul-
sive curiosity. The landlady said "Beat it," and shut the
door in their faces, but they only wandered back to
stare further at the ambulance.

Up above now, in the open windows of the surrounding tenements, new faces had appeared, and eyes
were riveted on the doorway of the yellow brick building. No one talked, no one moved away, and no one
came down. Only two adults were on the street, and
they had been there before the ambulance came — a
dumpy, elderly woman, and the black janitor of a
neighboring tenement.

When the two men had gone into the house, one
of the boys, a wiry, sallow-faced, blond lad, jerked his
thumb and murmured softly to the others: "Oh, mamma, ain't they got the job?"

"They'll be carrying *you* down some day, Shorty,"
a stoutish lad commented with an attempt at humor.

"Knock on wood," the blond one replied, tapping
his knuckles on his head.

"Here comes Big-Feet Mary," a third lad an-

nounced, pointing. Inspired by an idea, he doubled over
with silent, exaggerated laughter. "Let's tell her we got
a customer to play bingo."

The boys watched Mary's approach. They felt affection for Mary because she was coarsely good-
hearted, letting them play freely in front of her basement flat, occasionally treating them to a taste of beer.
Yet their affection was blended with contempt because
Mary was a queer one, a funny-looking, offbeat gal.
Widowed, and the mother of four little girls, Mary el-
bowed her way through life by turning a penny from
the minor sins of her neighbors. She ran a private bingo
party twice a week for all who enjoyed a game of
chance, and anyone else she could wheedle into coming. In addition, she augmented her penny profits by the
illicit, tax-free liquor she procured from time to time
and sold to friends she could trust. She always was in
danger of a collision with the law, but her four little
girls were tolerably well fed and neat as a pin.

Mary clumped down the street, stomping as always
like a big truck horse striking sparks from cobble-
stones. The nickname "Big Feet" did not come from
the size of her feet, which were not out of the ordinary,
but from the noise she made in walking. This in turn
was the result of the metal cleats worn on her heels to
preserve shoe leather. Now, with a genial, fleshy grin on
her rubicund face, Mary clip-clopped toward the ambulance. She had stumpy legs like the supports of an
old-fashioned sofa, her figure was barrel round, and
her bottom was gargantuan. At thirty-five she was quite

a thing to see walking and the boys met her, as always, with suppressed giggles.

"Hello," Mary chirped to them, waving her hand. "Hello, Tommy, hello, Dusty, hello, boys." Her voice had a warm, coarse, throaty quality.

Dusty, a stocky lad of twelve, winked at his fellows, shoved his hands into the pockets of his trousers, and began the game: "Hey, Mary, we got somebody wants to play bingo."

"Yes?" Mary inquired, all alertness. She gazed from one to the other. "Where is he?"

"It ain't a man, it's a woman."

"Did you give her my address? Did you tell her when we play? Did you talk me up?" Mary inquired eagerly.

"No, but I'll introduce you when she comes down. She's right upstairs."

"For heaven's sake," said Mary, "I don't need introductions. I just talk to people."

"You'll need an introduction to this dame," the Italian lad put in with a guffaw.

The boys laughed. Mary paused, looking alertly from one to the other — and then for the first time noted the presence of the ambulance. She asked quickly, "What's this here for?"

"Just somebody visiting somebody," Dusty replied with a straight face.

"You sure?"

Several of the boys nodded.

"Well, give your friend my address," Mary said,

and then clip-clopped over to the two adults in the
doorway of the next building. "Hello, dearie," she said
to the woman, "I didn't see you in my place last night."
The woman, who was chewing on a piece of thread, was
in her late sixties, dressed in black, her eyes rheumy, a
dark mustache on her pallid face. "No, I guess I wasn't
there," she murmured. Then with odd irrelevance,
"Things is so dear."

"But bingo ain't dear," Mary argued sweetly.
"You win at bingo."

"I don't win. And my husband wallops me."

"But you can't never win if you don't play," Mary
persisted. "Bring your husband too."

"Well, I can't talk about it now," the woman replied with an air of great preoccupation. "Don't you
know there's a suicide in there?"

"A suicide?" Mary exclaimed with intense dismay.
"But there was one last week."

"That was only an old man — but this is a young
girl. And they're going to bring her down right away."

"Right away?" Mary echoed. Her ruddy face had
become liverish and she suddenly looked ill.

"Some of them plans it for weeks," the janitor said
reflectively. "This one had it all planned, I bet."

Sucking her thread, the woman in black replied
with disdain, "Them that kills themselves is crazy."

"They ain't crazy," the janitor argued, "they's sorrowful."

One of the drivers suddenly appeared. He stepped
into the front cab of the ambulance and leaned over the
seat. He pulled out a canvas tarpaulin, so folded that it

looked like a market bag with handles at its top. Walking at an even pace, with no particular expression on his face, he reentered the building.

"That's for to wrap the body with," the elderly woman exclaimed with animation. She chewed her black thread vigorously. "I wonder what she looks like now?"

"Oh don't tell me," Mary cried, backing away. "A young girl! Oh, I don't want to stay here any more." She clumped off quickly across the street — but there paused, gazing up with pained wonder at the dark-shaded window of the rooming house.

"Hey, Mary," the stout boy called to her, "aintcha gonna wait for your customer?"

Mary didn't reply, but she looked over at him reproachfully.

"She's real crazy for bingo," Dusty jibed, "only you're gonna hafta lay her down to rest once in a while. She ain't so strong."

"And you ain't so funny neither," the blond boy murmured suddenly out of the corner of his mouth. "Why don't you let ol' Mary alone?"

"What's it to you?"

"You're a jerk," the blond boy replied sharply. "Shut up or I'll slam you down."

The door of the rooming house opened again and conversation stopped. Both men came out. They walked to the rear of the ambulance and opened the doors. Inside all was dazzling white, excessively sanitary-looking. Piled one on the other were several unpainted pine boxes without covers. The men lifted out the topmost one. The children became very still, even the youngest ones ceasing their chatter. The man who was holding the rear of the box rested it for a moment on his hip and thigh, while using his free hand to close the door. They went inside with the smaller youngsters trailing after them. The landlady shut the door and leaned against the jamb with folded arms. "Beat it," she said. She was a slatternly woman with gray streaking her muddy brown hair. "There's nothin' to see, so now get away," she told them with weary harshness.

The little ones scurried a few feet back. They gazed avidly at the shut door.

"Hey!" the stout lad announced humorously as he jerked his thumb at the ambulance, "It's nice in there."

The blond boy shook his head. "Oh, you jerk!"

"Oh ashes to ashes," the lad in blue denim recited, "Oh ashes to ashes, and ashes to ashes, and ashes to ashes . . ."

"I know that one," a red-haired girl burst out. "Ashes to ashes and dust to dust . . ."

"Shut your face or I'll give you a bust," the Italian lad said. The boys laughed quietly.

"I wish they'd hurry up and bring her down," the stout one murmured. "I gotta go home for dinner."

The blond boy clapped a hand to his face. "Oh mamma, he's thinking of eating. What a jerk!"

The other snickered, "This ain't the first stiff I ever seen. Maybe you never seen one, but I seen plenty."

"Bet you never saw what I saw," the Italian lad burst out excitedly. "I saw a man carved up like this"

— he sliced his finger across his middle. "Oh boy, don't ask, did I have nightmares!"

"Listen," another began —

The landlady opened the door. "They're coming," a little towhead of six cried out in an excess of excitement. He bounced up and down. "They're bringing the box." He scurried back, his fair skin flushed, his blue eyes feverish.

A hush descended on the street. The two adults in the next doorway moved out for a better view. The woman in black stopped chewing her bit of thread; it hung wetly over her lower lip. Those in the windows of the surrounding houses leaned forward. Then, before the men could emerge, Big-Feet Mary uttered a curious, muffled cry. Her face became blood-red. She turned her back and started away furiously, clip-clopping down the street. She did not look back, nor did the others turn to watch her go. Her shoes pounded loudly until she stepped down to her basement flat and disappeared. Then the street became silent again.

The men appeared. The box had its anonymous occupant now in its dark, canvas shroud. The younger children stared in eager fascination, but it was clear that they could not fully comprehend. The older boys, clumped together, looked on intensely, lips pressed together. The blond boy quickly crossed himself.

The man holding the front of the box rested it on his hip and thigh with practiced ease while he opened the door latch with one hand. Without a word both men strained in unison, lifting the heavy burden, sliding it

in. The doors closed. With impassive faces, the two men
walked to the front. The motor started, the ambulance
pulled away.

The silence broke then, abruptly. On the sidewalk,
where the younger children were standing, a small girl
bounced her rubber ball, swung a leg over it skillfully,
and commenced counting, "One, two, button my shoe,"
as though the day were as usual again, and nothing
had really happened. The towhead shrieked and burst
into chatter.

The older boys, clumped together in the middle of
the street, were still quiet. The intense looks, the
strained eyes, had not wholly relaxed. They shuffled
around, hands in pockets. "Oh mamma," the blond boy
murmured, "there she goes. Another stiff gone to hell!"

The stout one spat. "That's the way it is. I'm used
to it."

"Who wants to play some ball?" Dusty asked
quietly.

"Okay," another murmured.

"Cripes, look!" the blond boy exclaimed, pointing
to the door of the rooming house. "She don't waste no
time, does she?"

The landlady had hung a sign behind the glass
pane of the front door. It said "Vacancy."

The Italian kid clapped his hands together. "Oh,
ashes to ashes . . . Oh, ashes to ashes, and ashes to
ashes, and ashes to ashes . . ."

The blond lad spit and laughed softly.

Presently they began to play ball.

Afternoon
in the Jungle

Afternoon
in the Jungle

Charles Fallon, aged thirteen, jiggled a hand grenade in his palm and waited for the traffic lights to change. When the Eighth Avenue bus moved off, he took cover behind a snow pile. At twenty yards he looped the deadly missile high into the air. It exploded squarely on top of the bus. Charlie smiled with satisfaction and scooped up snow for another grenade.

He progressed slowly up Hudson Street, killing time, a smallish, wiry, rather white-faced boy with tight

"Afternoon in the Jungle" was first published in 1941.

109

lips. At the corner of Perry he found an envelope containing one million two hundred and thirty-four dollars. He dropped his grenade and crossed the avenue to a pawnshop. It was Sunday, and there was a steel-mesh gate in front of the door, but Charlie made a wish and got inside. He helped himself to a flashlight, a pair of ice-skates, a Boy Scout knife, binoculars, a picture of Mary in the Manger, and a lot of other things. He left a hundred-thousand-dollar bill in payment.

At Twelfth Street he crossed the avenue again. He wandered down Greenwich, stopping to gaze at the pictures in the lobby of a movie house. He decided that Anita Louise was nicer-looking than a stuck-up like Norma Shearer. He kissed Anita Louise. They sat on the edge of her million-dollar swimming pool, and he kissed her again. She was about to tell him how swell he was when the ticket-taker came over and said, "Beat it, kid." He scuffed away.

At Eleventh Street and Seventh Avenue he planted himself before the window of a bakery. In rapid succession he ate a chocolate cake, a napoleon, a charlotte russe, and two twenty-five cent peach cakes with whipped cream. He was just about to buy the whole bakery when a lady came out and told him to stop leaning against the glass and move along.

Bored, he turned down Seventh Avenue and started home. Between Commerce and Morton he went into a candy store where he occasionally traded. The stout proprietress wheezed over to the counter.

"How much is the caramels?" Charlie asked.

"Two for a penny."

"And these?"

"Four for a penny."

"And the lollipops?"

"A penny apiece. Which do you want?"

"I'm going home and get some money. I'll be back in eight minutes."

He crossed the street again and walked down to Houston, wishing he could buy some candy. He knew a way to make one caramel last half an hour. You put it on your tongue and sucked it. It took willpower not to chew it right down, but the sweet taste stayed with you longer. And you avoided the toothache. He took off his soaking mittens and blew on his hands. He wished it weren't Sunday. His neighborhood was like a cemetery on Sunday because the factories were closed.

A bus approached, going south. Old Man Sheehy and his wife, who lived in Charlie's house, ran across Varick to catch it. The bus stopped. The old couple hurried forward and, as Mr. Sheehy took his hand from his pocket, a fifty-cent piece dropped to the sidewalk. He made a frantic grab for it, but the coin rolled onto the subway grille and dropped to the bottom of the pit. Muttering, the old man stepped up into the bus. He held the door back with his hand and shouted out to Charlie, who had run over to the grille, "If you find it, Charlie, I'll give you a dime!"

"Sure," said Charlie.

The bus moved off, and Charlie raced away. He would need chewing gum and a string to do the lifting. Fifty cents! He had retrieved pennies from subway grilles — once even a dime — but this was the first chance he had ever had at so much money. It would be the simplest thing in the world, of course, to tell Old Man Sheehy that he had not been able to find it.

He covered the distance to his house on Downing Street at a run. He was too excited to remember the broken step on the second flight of stairs, and his right foot slipped through, flinging him headlong and giving him a terrible crack on the shin. He limped up the remaining three flights with tears in his eyes.

His mother was sitting at the window, darning.

"Ma, can I *please* have three pennies?" he asked. Phrased as a question, his words expressed a command. He had learned long ago that his mother always yielded to bullying.

"Hush, for goodness!" she said. "Your father's asleep. Now, why do you come in here with your wet rubbers and filthy the floor?"

"I'm going right out again. Just give me the pennies, Ma."

"I can't give you pennies. You had a penny for candy on Tuesday."

"Ma, I got to have them. Look, there's a dime that fell down in the subway place. If I had some chewing gum I could get it up."

"So that's it? You were trying to hold out on me, weren't you?" She laughed softly. "I'll give you one penny, not three, and you'll have to give it back."

"One's no good. I gotta have three. I can't do anything with one. It doesn't make a big enough piece of gum, don't you see, Ma?"

Mrs. Fallon went into the kitchen and came back with her change purse. "I only have two pennies," she said. "Beside a dime for church tonight."

"Well, give me that. I'll . . ." He stopped to sneeze, "I'll change it. You'll get it all back, honest."

"No. I can't risk it." She gave him the two pennies.

Glumly Charlie accepted them. This would make his task harder, but he knew that his mother was inflexible about church money as about nothing else.

"And I expect the two pennies back," she said.

"O.K." He was already busy in the kitchen, searching for a string.

"Ah, yes," his mother said, in the long-suffering whine he knew so well, "in the old days if you'd come to your father or me for a penny we'd given you a nickel. If you'd asked for a nickel you'd get a dime."

Charlie found a ball of heavy cord, cut off a ten-foot length, and stuffed it quickly into his pocket.

"But now your father's a cripple, poor man," his mother went on. "Limping where other men walk, working at night when other men work at day, he's grateful for the little he has."

"O.K., Ma, I'm going," said Charlie. Without waiting for an answer, he banged out. He told himself that all mothers were a pain and fathers worse. Catch the old man giving up a glass of beer to buy his kid a chocolate bar.

He ran down the block and around the corner to the candy store on Carmine Street. He bought two boxes of Chiclets and emptied them both into his mouth. The gum had to be moist and pliable or else the coin wouldn't stick to it. He trotted across Varick, chewing hard but on the right side of his mouth only, so that he wouldn't get a toothache. Near the bus sign he lay down full length on the icy grille. The concrete base at the bottom of the pit was covered with debris and snow and little puddles of water. Methodically he began to search for the coin, inching himself along from one spot to another on the grille. His heart pumped with excitement, and an image of the bakery window danced in his head.

Ten minutes passed with no result, and he stopped to blow on his hands. Then he returned to his task.

He located the coin. It lay half in a puddle of water, half on the concrete base — a difficult target. With a tight little smile on his lips he knotted the end of his cord several times and wound the chewing gum around the knot, giving it a broad, flat base. A wrist loop at the other end of the cord prevented his losing it. Then, after thrusting the wad of gum into his mouth for a last moistening, he lowered it carefully to the bottom.

Working intently, he did not notice the man who had come up behind him, a small, shabby man of about forty-five whose thin face was reddened by the wind but was liverish gray beneath the surface color.

Charlie heard him before he saw him; the man's breathing was labored as though he were straining at a heavy burden. The boy looked up briefly and went back to his work. He was concentrating upon the most difficult part of his job. The wad of gum was not sufficiently heavy to make a plumb line, yet he had to drop it with some force on the coin in order to make it take hold. It might take a hundred trials to achieve one accurate strike.

The man watched in silence for a moment. Then he dropped to his knees by Charlie's side, exclaiming in a hoarse tone, "Fifty cents, eh?" He peered down at the swaying length of cord above the coin. "Ah, it's hard that way, isn't it?" he asked softly.

Charlie didn't answer.

The man peered down to watch another trial. "Sure, the gum gets solid right away in this cold. It don't look to me like you'll make it, kid. And it's getting dark. You need real tools for this job. You'll never get it this way."

Without looking up, Charlie said loudly, "Who's asking you?"

The man got to his feet. Quickly he glanced all around. There was no one in sight. He stepped back a few paces and unbuttoned his overcoat. Secured to the inside of his coat by leather straps were four lengths of broom handle, whittled to reduced their thickness, each about three feet long, each fitted at one end with a rubber socket by which it could be joined to another length. With practiced efficiency he connected them. At the tip of the final length there was a small, rubber suction cup. He stepped forward, fitted the end of his pole neatly into the grate, and, dropping to his knees, thrust it to the bottom. "I'll show you how a professional does it," he said lightly. He kept his eyes averted from the boy's face. "Now, this is one method. Another is cup grease. With cup grease you can pick up a bracelet. But when you spot some change a suction cup is . . ."

"What's the idea?" Charlie cried out in fury. "What do you think you're doing?"

"I'll show you how a professional does it, kid."

"Get out of here!" With his left hand Charlie tugged savagely at the man's arm. "Get out of here!"

The man fended him off, laughing in a hoarse tone that had no humor in it. "What's the difference? You wouldn't get it," he said. "Why let it lay there for somebody else?"

"The hell I won't get it!" Charlie cried. "You leave it alone. It's mine. Please, mista."

"I'll give you a nickel," said the man.

Charlie pulled up his string with decision and crammed it into his pocket. Then, rising, he stepped behind the man and kicked him viciously in the small of his back. The man cried out in pain. Instantly Charlie retreated a dozen feet.

"That's a hell of a thing to do," the man groaned, holding his back. "I'll break your neck, you little rat. You almost made me drop my pole." They glared at each other for a moment, motionless and undecided. There were thirty years between them, yet in a way they looked startlingly alike. Both were small, the boy as boy, the man as man; both were drawn, hard-bitten.

The man knelt down again, watching Charlie carefully. He lowered the pole, but kept his head raised. Charlie stood indecisively. Then he ran to a snow pile by the curbstone. The man shifted to face him. "You come near me and I'll break your neck," he said. "I'm telling you. Beat it. I won't even give you the nickel now. I 'm mad."

Charlie grabbed a chunk of ice from the snow pile. He flung it with all his strength. It missed by a foot, but the man was frightened and jumped to his feet, pulling up the pole. Charlie retreated behind the snow pile. Trembling, eyes fixed on his enemy, he clawed under the crust of ice.

"You're looking for trouble, ain't you?" the man said bitterly. He glanced up and down the deserted, darkening avenue. "You think I like this?" he asked suddenly. "Do you think I like to fight with a kid like you over fifty cents?"

A snowball struck his knee just below the protection of his frayed overcoat. He shook his fist, his voice swelling with anger. "I'll give you trouble if you want it, you kid!" He stopped, panting for breath. Then he dropped the pole and hurled himself forward. Charlie darted out of reach. A snowball, almost pure ice, struck the man full in the forehead. He slapped a hand to his head, half sobbing in rage and pain.

"How do you like that, you skunk?" the boy cried.

The man chased him, but Charlie was twice as agile and kept the snow barrier between them. Within a minute the man stopped, his mouth open, a hand pressed to his heaving chest. Without uttering a word, he went back to the grille and crouched down, lowering his pole.

Frantic, the boy varied his attack. He came past at an angling run, from behind, and slammed down a piece of loose ice. It struck the man at the base of his neck. His body quivered, but he didn't turn. He was raising the pole to slip it through another opening in the grille. Charlie made another rush, this time determined to use his feet. Swearing, the man leaped up to meet him, catching the boy's arm as he veered off in terror and swinging him in. He had him gripped by both arms. The pole lay on the grille between them.

"I ought to break your neck!" he cried, shaking him. "I ought to break your ratty little neck! But I'm not going to, see? You're a kid. But you listen . . ."

Charlie twisted hard, broke free, and at the same moment stamped on the man's foot. He ran to the security of the snow pile. The man stood looking at him blankly, his face twisted in pain. "Oh Jesus," he cried, "what a little gutter rat! Did I hurt you? Did I do anything to you when I had the chance? I was going to make you a proposition." A snowball struck him in the chest. "All right," he said. "I can't get it if you don't let me. You can't get it if I don't let you. We're both going to lose it. It's getting dark. I'll split with you. I'll give you twenty-five cents."

"No!" Charlie cried. "It's mine!" His whole body was shaking.

"Don't you see you can't get it without real tools?" The man was pleading now. "Your gum ain't no good in this cold weather."

"It's mine."

"Jesus, you found it, I'll admit it," the man said. "But I got a suction cup. I can get it for both of us."

"No."

"Jesus Christ, I got to have some of it!" the man

cried, his voice corroded by shame and bitterness. "This is my *business,* kid. It's all I do. Can't you understand? I been walking all day. I ain't found a thing. You got to let me have some of it. You got to!"

"No."

The man flung out his hands. "Oh, you kid, you kid!" he cried despairingly. "If you was ten years older you'd understand. Do you think I like to do this? If you was ten years older I could talk to you. You'd understand.

Charlie's lips tightened. His white face, spotted by the cold, was filled with rage. "If I was ten years older I'd beat your face in," he said.

The man bent painfully and picked up the pole. Limping slightly, his hand pressed to the small of his back, he walked away. He was crying.

Charlie stood trembling in triumph, his face turned to stone.

It had become dark.

Circus
Come
to Town

Circus
Come
to Town

At seven forty-five in the morning the two brothers reached the circus grounds to discover that the circus had not yet arrived. The immense, grassy field was barren of tents, of ladies in spangled tights, of elephants

---

"Circus Come to Town" was first published in 1950.

and freaks, and all else that town lore associated with a circus. Alan, aged seven, permitted himself a frank wail of disappointment: "Maybe it isn't gonna come!"

Eddie, who was twelve, replied calmly, "The posters said Saturday, didn't they? Don't be a goof." He added after a moment's reflection, "It's good we're early, we'll be sure to get hired, see? First come, first hired."

"They'll hire *me*, won't they, Eddie?"

Eddie yearned to reply, "How many times you gonna ask me that, you goof? How do I know?" Instead, since he was himself acutely worried by the same problem, he answered, "I'll get you a job. You just let me do the asking."

"You sure there'll be clowns?"

"There's always clowns."

"How do you know?"

"I know, that's all." Eddie took his Boy Scout knife from his pocket and opened a blade. "Let's play mumbley-peg. It'll kill time."

"The clowns I wanna see most," Alan murmured. "Them and the cannon that shoots people. It'll be awful if it don't come."

They sat cross-legged on the grass and began to play. The day was windy but fine; the sun was already warm, the air fragrant with the spring odors of turned soil, first hay cuttings and wild flowers.

Except for a difference in height and weight the two brothers were much alike in appearance. Both were towheads, fair of skin and blue-eyed, with lean, delicately boned faces; both were slender, wiry, and

thin of body. Their family resemblance was further ac-
cented by their clothes: the same faded, worn, and
patched denim trousers; the sleeveless, cotton shirts of
identical cut, although different hue; the sneakers
scuffed at the sides and patched with adhesive tape.
They played their game and chattered about the circus
— and secretly worried. Eddie had never seen a large
circus, and Alan had not seen any circus at all, and
there was great question in their minds whether they
would see this one today.

They lived in a small Indiana hamlet in the center
of a farming area. It was a "play-date" considered by
circus people to be worth a visit only once in several
years. When the posters that advertised the one-day,
gigantic spectacle had first appeared, the boys had
rushed to their mother with the news. She had listened
to them as she always did and replied, as she so often
did, "I'm sorry, kids, but two tickets cost a dollar twenty cents and I just don't have it for circuses." There had
been no argument from the boys. Since the day, three
years before, that their father had deserted his family,
the words "no" and "I'm sorry" had come to live with
them and be accepted.

But shortly after this conversation Eddie had
learned something momentous from an older boy. If
you came early, if you carried water or helped set up
seats or did other work, you were given a free pass.
And so here they were at seven forty-five, the two
Campbell brothers with two peanut butter sandwiches
in a paper bag, both of them passionately eager to go
to work. But their work had not yet arrived, and they

had reason to be worried. With Alan it was the dark, gnawing question of whether a seven-year-old would be hired at all; but for Eddie it was something else. On days when their mother was away at work he was responsible for his brother. She had permitted this expedition on the sole condition that he would not separate himself from the younger boy. He had promised — but he had an ugly premonition: that he alone would be hired and would therefore have to choose between the circus and his duty. To forego the circus was unthinkable; but to let Alan manage himself for the day and walk the mile home alone would mean a licking and bed without supper. And so Eddie was playing mumbley-peg with a sense that no matter what he decided some sort of disaster was lying in wait for him.

Eight o'clock became eight-thirty, became nine. More and more boys appeared at the field. The Campbells stopped playing their game and circulated like spies in an enemy land. Each newcomer was asked whether he was buying a circus ticket or working to get in. And each new rival for employment, of whom there were a good many, was estimated as to age, strength, and potential competition on the labor market.

Finally at ten-thirty the first heralds of glory arrived, a line of trailers pulled by roaring tractors. The huge trailers were painted red and had "Berry Bros. Circus" inscribed in white on their sides. A great, ecstatic shout burst from the throats of all the waiting boys and they raced down the length of the field yelling, "I'll work . . . hire me . . . I'm strong." No one hired them and no one paid any attention to them beyond shouting occasionally, "Look-out there . . . watch out now . . . stand back." More and more trailers arrived and were dispersed to separate portions of the field. Then several station wagons appeared and from them issued a swarm of men in overalls and jeans who leaped into feverish activity. Some lowered the sides of the trailers, disclosing great bundles of canvas and immense, vari-colored poles; others climbed upon the tractors to operate lifting winches and mechanical stake-drivers.

The Campbell boys, like the others, scurried from one spot of activity to the other and called eagerly in thin, boy voices, "You want some help? . . . Will you hire me? . . . You want some kids?" They were waved away or shouted away by men who were not unfriendly, but who were behind schedule and furiously preoccupied. And as more trailers appeared and more men — and then a fantastic, lumbering line of fourteen trotting elephants, each holding with its trunk the tail of the elephant ahead — and as the canvas was unrolled and spread on the ground, with even a few of the elephants put to work at pulling and hauling — despair gripped the brothers. Alan cried, "They ain't gonna hire us, you'll see, it's just a fakey story." Eddie, wanting to reassure him, needed reassurance himself and could offer his brother no comfort. It seemed to both of them unaccountable and malicious that useful boys were not hired when there was so much activity on the field and so much work to be done.

And still the tractors roared off and returned with

more trailers and more men. Presently the field became a dangerous place for small boys. They were warned loudly and repeatedly to beat it. In gloomy silence they wandered down to a quiet corner where the non-working elephants had been lined up, side by side. There they found other boys and compared notes and learned that no one at all had been hired. They sat down and watched the elephants and watched the activity on the field and became increasingly gloomy.

"I told you," Alan muttered after a while. "They don't want kids. Let's go home."

"Home? What for? This is more fun than home."

"No it ain't. Not if we can't see the circus."

"We're seein' elephants, ain't we? Why don't you look at the elephants?"

"I'm tired of the elephants. I wanna see the clowns. If I can't see the clowns, I don't wanna stay."

"Well, you can't go home! I'll give you a bat on the ear if you go home."

Alan's voice turned shrill. "You don't dare hit me, I'll tell Ma."

"Aw, listen, don't be a baby. I'm not gonna hit you. But what do you wanna go home for? It's better here. There's still time to get hired, ain't there?"

"I wanna see the clowns," Alan muttered.

It turned eleven o'clock. Their paper bag was opened, and the two peanut butter sandwiches were devoured. By now there were many more boys sitting with them on the edge of the field and a sprinkling of adults also. Rumors passed along the line: The circus had arrived late, and for this reason there would be no afternoon show, and no boys would be hired. And following this a story exactly the opposite: In order to make the afternoon performance extra help was needed. Every boy who wanted to work would be hired at twelve o'clock and would be paid a dollar in addition to his free ticket. "You see," Eddie cried triumphantly, "I told you to wait." Alan was cheered by this but when twelve o'clock came and no one was hired he began again to mutter about going home.

Presently a good-sized tent was raised at one corner of the field and word passed that it was the cookhouse for the circus people and that boys would be needed to set up tables and benches. But no one came to hire them and when several of the older boys walked out on the field to inquire, they were waved off immediately. The menagerie tent went up, the walls billowing in the wind, and then the sideshow tent and then, at one o'clock, the immense big top was raised and a shout went up from the spectators, because it was an exciting sight — but there was no work for the Campbells or for any other boy. There was only the grim spectacle of several circus workers who came to drive stakes into the ground at intervals all along the edge of the field. They hammered the stakes and looped them with rope and walked away.

The brothers sat on the ground, close together, silent. For three weeks they had drenched their hearts in the glory and drama of this day. It had turned very sour. And when, after another half hour of waiting, a boy sitting near them rose to his feet, announcing loudly that he thought he'd see if the sideshow was open for ticket-buyers, they turned and looked upon his departing back as upon a personal enemy and then turned and gazed at each other in bleak misery, each comprehending for the first time in his young life the full and terrible power of money.

And then they were hired. Suddenly, standing before them was a big, cheerful-looking man in a soiled, blue-serge suit, his gay tie flapping a little in the wind, his straw Panama hat pushed back on his balding head. He whistled shrilly with two fingers in his mouth, laughed as the line of boys started in surprise and bawled loudly, "Any you kids wanna see the circus?" Some eighty boys from five to sixteen jumped to their feet, all screaming "yes" at the same time. The man laughed, whistled piercingly again to bring silence, and then said, "I kinda thought so. Come around close." The boys ducked under the rope and thronged about him. He pointed suddenly at Alan. "You sonny — how old are you?"

Alan stammered, quickly slipped into a lie, "Eight."

"That's good. I just wanted to be sure you were over two; we don't hire no kids under two."

A gale of appreciative laughter came from the boys. The man laughed with them, then abruptly sobered and whistled quickly for silence. He gazed at them with a measure of severity now, but with a lingering grin at the corners of his wide, thin mouth. "Listen to me careful, boys. No more joking." He held up a purple card. "When show time comes, I'm gonna give every one of you boys one of these tickets. That'll get you in free. All you gonna do for me is help pull a few ropes, 'cause it's a windy day, an' then set up some seats. You'll work maybe an hour, hour an' a half." He pointed at Alan again. "Now nobody expects you to be as strong as a big boy. If you were all big boys, it'd be better for me, but you ain't. But so long as you do your share you'll get a ticket."

"I'll do it," Alan cried passionately.

"I'll do it," a five-year-old echoed.

"Okay. Now you boys are lucky today, awful lucky. Some days we make good train connections an' we set up early an' we only have work for twenty or thirty. But today we're late an' we're gonna use every one of you." He paused while the boys cheered. "But you listen to me. Square is square. I know all the tricks. I been sixteen years with the circus and I been pushing boys for nine. That's my name. Pusher. You want to know anything, yell for Pusher. Now there's some boys who'll work twenty minutes an' then duck under a tent flap. They come back later wanting a ticket but they don't get it. There's other boys haven't got no fair play an' they wanna quit before show time. They don't get a ticket neither. There's still other boys who ain't even here, but they'll show up two hours from now an' claim they worked like you did. Only they don't know me. Square is square. I don't give free tickets for nothing. An' you know why I'm the pusher? Because I remember faces. I been studying every one of your faces an' there isn't no boy gonna claim he was here unless I see him with my own two eyes right now. You got that?"

The boys shouted that they understood and were ready.

"Come on then." Grinning a little, he started off at a dogtrot for the menagerie tent. The Campbell brothers, eyes shining with glory and delight, kept close together in the swarm of running boys. When they reached the tent, a distance of forty yards or so, Pusher's chest was heaving and the sweat was rolling from his temples down the sides of his meaty face. He said with a cheerful laugh, "I sure can't run . . . like you boys . . . can. But you got it now . . . we're awful late. Bad rain last night . . . " He wagged a stubby forefinger at them and suddenly roared: "You get it? No show this afternoon unless you work hard and fast. I wanna see you go at the double." He thrust two fingers into his mouth, whistled piercingly and yelled, "Larry, where the hell are you on the guy ropes, Larry?"

A youngish man, unshaven, hair tousled, in dirty, khaki coveralls, came running out of the menagerie tent. Pusher pointed accusingly at the flapping canvas and asked with anger, "You want it to blow down? I told you to start pulling ropes."

"Can't do everything," the other replied sullenly. "Joe said to spread hay for the antelopes."

"What's the matter with that Joe? Is he married to one of those antelopes? I wouldn't be surprised. Tight those ropes up before she blows away, goddammit. You kids here" — he gestured with both arms to a group of six boys that included the Campbells — "you stick with my friend, Larry. Do what he tells you."

"Wait a minute, how about some heft here?" Larry

asked sullenly. There was a husky fifteen-year-old boy in the group, but the others were all younger. "How about some beef?"

"This ain't the only tent, an' I gotta start those chairs in. You think five thousand chairs move in by themselves?" He turned to the boys. "When you get finished here, come over to the big top, I'll give you your tickets . . . c'mon kids." Pusher ran off, the other boys dogtrotting behind him.

"Oh boy, oh boy," Alan whispered to his brother with swollen pride, "I told you I wouldn't be too little."

"Work hard now," Eddie advised. "We gotta keep on the good side of 'em."

Larry said with mingled acidity and humor, "All right, you day-laborers, three on each side of that guy rope, smallest boys close to me." The group of boys took position and eagerly grasped the heavy rope. Larry bent over the low stake, deftly slipped the knot by which the rope, running from stake to tent wall, was fastened. He snagged the loose end in a hitch around the stake, held it with both hands. "All right, hit it!" The boys pulled hard and Larry jerked. "Hit it!" They pulled again, watching the tent wall become tauter. "Hit it hard! Hold it!" Quickly he looped the rope around the stake, tied it off. He moved to the next stake. As they waited for him to slip the knot, Alan whispered excitedly to Eddie, who was alongside of him, "Ask him if there's trained dogs in the show."

"Sh! We don't wanna bother him."

The command came, "Hit it!" They pulled. "Hit it . . . Hit it hard . . . Hold!"

They moved from the second stake to the third, to a fourth, a fifth. And rather quickly, for both brothers, the pleasure departed from what they were doing. It was work, hard work, to pull down mightily on a thick, manila rope with the tent wall snapping away in the wind. This was rope that had been weathered and beaten by sun and rain and time. Hempen barbs pricked and scratched their flesh, and their soft boy-palms began to be chafed. Alan's arms commenced to feel heavy, his fingers to ache. The double line of stakes around the large tent seemed endless and Larry's command kept up without pause: "Hit it! Hit it! Hit it hard!"

"My hands hurt," Alan burst out suddenly.

"Spit on 'em," Larry advised. "Don't let 'em get hot."

The boys all spat on their palms and went back to work with a heightened morale that did not last long. There was no magic in spitting on one's palms, they found. The flesh continued to redden and became increasingly sore and they were pulling a little less hard and taking a bit longer with each rope. "C'mon, lean on it," Larry was beginning to say. "Hit it, will ya?"

They became lost in a jungle of ropes and stakes. Breathing became labored and lids blinked as salt sweat trickled into the corners of their eyes; thighs trembled with strain; soft young bodies, accustomed to hard play but not to sustained work, yearned for rest. "Hit it! Hit it hard!"

Eddie Campbell, panting and weary, began to worry. Knowing his own fatigue, he was afraid for his brother. If Alan stopped work, he would be fired. And if that happened, what would *he* do? Suddenly, although he was afraid of Larry, he asked boldly, "Mista, can't we stop for a minute?"

Larry straightened up, laughed a little, not unsympathetically, and said, "Only half around, kids."

The oldest boy amongst them, who was fifteen, spat on his square hands and said boastfully, "I'm not tired."

"Well, if you're not, I am," Larry told him. "Sure, take a breather." He threw back his head and stared up at the serene blue of the sky and said with a laugh, "Anybody works in a circus oughta have his head examined. I sure hate a windy day, rather have rain than wind."

"How you doin'?" Eddie whispered anxiously to his brother.

"I'm awful tired," the latter confessed.

"I'm tired, too, but you're not gonna stop workin', are you?"

"Oh no, I wanna see the clowns."

"That's the boy."

"Do *your* hands hurt, Eddie? Mine hurt awful. I'm gettin' blisters, look."

"Mine hurt too, but you won't stop workin', will you? We done half already."

"Oh no, I won't stop."

One of the other boys asked, "Mista, you know what time it is?"

"A little past two about. Let's go, kids."

"The show starts at two-thirty, don't it?"

"Never has so far this season. My guess is today it'll start about four."

"You think maybe we can see the sideshow then, the freaks 'n everything?" Alan asked eagerly. "Does the ticket give us that, too?"

"I don't know, I ain't running this damn circus," Larry answered tartly. "C'mon hit it! Hit it! Hit it hard!"

They worked and Alan's weariness turned into fatigue, fatigue into aching exhaustion. He heard Eddie's whispered, panting encouragement. "C'mon, kid, only a few more, kid," but he began to lose the power of response. Pride and desire could no longer weigh against burning hands and leaden arms. He stopped work.

"Oh, c'mon," Eddie pleaded fiercely, *"please."*

"I can't."

"You might as well sit down," Larry told him sullenly. "You ain't doin' no good anyway."

"You'll lose your ticket, Alan," his brother cried despairingly. "Let him keep working, Mister, *please.*"

"Oh, shoot, if that's what you're worried about, forget it," said Larry. "You think I'm gonna report you or something? What do you take me for?" He added to Alan, "You move along with us so Pusher don't spot you, that's all. C'mon, hit it, kids."

"Jeez, thanks," Eddie cried.

"Hit it! Hit it hard!"

The big tent was circled finally, all ropes snagged tight, the canvas secure against the wind. "Amen," said

Larry, "finished, wrapped up." He chuckled softly as he looked at the boys. The fifteen-year-old had borne the work well but the others were almost as dead beat as Alan; all of them, including Eddie, had blisters on their hands. "Pooped out, yeah?" Larry said with his wry grin. "Okay, hop over to Pusher an' get your tickets. I hope it was worth it."

"I ain't tired," the fifteen-year-old said boastfully. "I'm used to hard work."

"Well good for you, Sonny."

"Thanks, Mista," Eddie murmured. "About my brother, I mean."

Larry reached out and poked him in the ribs. "You do the same thing for me some day."

Alan asked, "Can we get some water someplace? I'm so thirsty!"

"See over there, by that small tent? There's a water bag. If you find any beer in it, whistle for me." Larry grinned and went back into the menagerie tent.

Slowly, but feeling the triumph of their accomplishment, the boys made their way across the field. They compared blisters and lied to one another that they were only a little tired. Alan whispered to his brother, "I did good, didn't I?"

"Sure you did."

"I wouldna stopped but my hands hurt so much."

"You did swell. You did great."

"Are *you* tired?"

"Yeah, a little."

The water was warm and tasted of the canvas

bag, but they gulped it with pleasure and relief. And then, somewhat revived, they started off at a quicker pace for the big top.

"I wished you'd asked him about the dogs," Alan said. "Next to the clowns I wanna see dogs climb ladders an' things. I hope they have dogs."

"I'll ask Pusher," Eddie replied. "He'll know."

They found Pusher near the big top. He was standing before a trailer directing a line of scurrying boys who were carrying chairs. They went up to him in a group, the fifteen-year-old boy in the lead. He said, "Pusher, here we are. We fixed the ropes. You got our tickets for us?"

"Course I have," Pusher replied cheerily. "Just grab some chairs now an' run 'em in, two boys to a team."

Eddie said in a faint voice, "You mean we gotta work some *more*?"

"We gotta run those seats in, don't we?" Pusher answered jovially. "Can't have a show without seats. Only half in yet. Let's go now, they ain't heavy."

"You said we'd get our tickets," the fifteen-year-old charged resentfully. "Why don't you give 'em to us?"

"Now look here," said Pusher with the smile vanishing from his face, "don't you tell me my business. My job's to get those seats in. I can't help it if there's a wind blows up an' we hafta pull ropes, too. A little double duty won't hurt you. My job is seats. Whatsamatter, you too lazy to run a few chairs in? Well, yes or no — yes or no?"

"Okay," the boy muttered.

"Well, grab a partner an' get in line. C'mon, you towheads. Brothers, ain't you? Get busy."

"We're tired," Eddie said. "Awful tired."

Pusher ruffled his hair. "Won't hurt you to get a little tired. You're a working man, ain't you?" He gave them both a little shove, pushing them into line before the trailer. "Circus gonna start in fifteen, twenty minutes."

Alan said to his brother in a wailing voice, "I can't do any more, Eddie, I'm too tired, my hands hurt too much."

"But it's only fifteen minutes. He said the chairs ain't heavy."

"I can't do *anything,* Eddie."

"Well listen," Eddie whispered desperately, "you can make believe, can't you? I'll carry them by myself, but you hold one end, you make believe."

"Well . . . maybe I can do that."

"Let's go," Pusher bawled cheerfully, "hustle 'em in. Got crowds of people outside waitin' to see the show."

The chairs were stacked in flat piles in the trailer — wooden, folding chairs attached in braces of three. A sweating circus worker stood inside the trailer and handed them down one at a time, rapidly, to a brawny sixteen-year-old. He in turn passed them to the teams of boys. Each team, with Pusher's cheerful tongue to whip it on, then ran on the double quick to the big top some twenty yards away.

"Let's get a little speed on. Awful late today.

Wouldn't wanna miss the show altogether, would you, kids? Come on brothers, your turn, grab a chair."

Eddie seized the chair-flat in both arms, and Alan lifted one end as high as his exhausted muscles could manage, and they both ran at a dogtrot with Pusher's voice lacing their backs. Panting they made the interior of the big top. It was an immense confusion of moving figures, contraptions being hoisted to the roof, men yelling, seats banging, and a uniformed band on a platform blowing discordant notes in tune-up. A voice called, "Well, don't stand there — move those seats, you kids." They followed the pointing arm of an assistant pusher to a rising tier of boards. They climbed the boards almost to the top where men were setting up seats. They delivered their burden and scrambled back down, dodging other teams going up, ducking away from a tractor. Eddie said, "Walk slow, we'll rest goin' back." They slowed down, and the voice of the assistant pusher cracked a whip over them. "Hey, you kids, you workin' or loafin'? No loafers here." They began again to run.

There had been a jungle of ropes and stakes and now there was a mountain of chair-flats. The trailer was emptied, but another trailer was ready by its side. The work was not physically as wearing as the ropes had been, and they could always rest a little on the return trip, yet they sustained it less well because they were more fatigued. Alan kept saying that he just had to sit down for a while, he had to — and Eddie kept pleading with him. "You'll get fired if you sit down. Look, I'm doin' all the carryin'. You wanna see the funny clowns, don't you? Don't you, Alan?" But he himself was rapidly becoming as exhausted as his brother. The faces of both of them were milky white with fatigue; their taffy hair was sodden.

It was Pusher who carried them through. They hated him bitterly, and that helped; they could not shut their ears to him and that also helped. "You see that feller? Wants a ticket for nothin'. He's tired, he says. Well ain't that too bad? Wants to work, but don't want to get a little tired. Well beat it, sonny. Just follow your nose an' beat it. You don't get no ticket from me. Now listen, you kids, the circus is gonna begin in another ten, fifteen, twenty minutes. If you want those nice little passes, you hustle them chairs. Only half a truck of chairs left now. Won't hurt you to work a little. It's good training, in fact, ha-ha. You hustle and I push, ha-ha, that's the way the world is. Move it, kids."

Eddie prayed. He prayed to dear God that Alan would not quit, that he himself would be able to hold out. He prayed that after all this hard work nothing, nothing would prevent them from seeing the circus.

When the last trailer was emptied and the last chair-flat set up, it was five minutes past four o'clock. Inside the big top the sawdust rings had been cleared, and the band was playing. The boys stood in line before Pusher waiting for their passes, and the bigger ones crowed wearily, "Guess we did a little work today, huh? . . . I'd sure like to travel with this circus." The younger boys stood in speechless fatigue, yet in final pride and triumph, while Pusher said in his cheery voice, "Any you kids wanna come back tonight at ten thirty an' move those chairs out again we'll give you a handful of change, a whole big handful of change. Well here you are kids, just like I said, go right in an' have a good time; you've never seen a circus like it!"

As in a dream the two brothers moved into the big top. The assistant pusher said, "Working boys, over there." They reached their section and found their seats and sat side by side, huddled, with glassy eyes. The tent was filling up, the band was playing with noisy verve, the spotlights glared down on the sawdust rings. Alan murmured, "The clowns, 'n' dogs, 'n' cannon, that's what I wanna see."

"The trapeze," Eddie muttered in reply.

They didn't talk more because they were beyond talk. They blinked their eyes against the lights and relaxed their spent bodies in the warmth of the sun-bathed tent. Presently the band began to play softly and an announcer's voice smote them from a microphone, but neither boy made much sense out of what he said. The band became brassy again and some Hindu dancing girls ran out from the wings. For what seemed a long time they whirled around before them and moved their arms to and fro like weaving snakes. The elephants came out and did things that they tried hard to watch, but they had seen the elephants already and the activity in all three rings was confusing. And presently, heads sagging on limp necks, the two brothers leaned against each other and fell asleep.

Pusher said, "Look at 'em. It never fails. I bet there's five kids up there sound asleep an' ten more don't know what they're seein'."

The assistant pusher said, "Well, you pushed 'em hard today, we were late."

"I pushed 'em? I didn't blow up that wind. I got my job to do, don't I? They wanna see the circus so bad they just beg you to work."

"What the hell, we got the matinee on; didn't think we'd make it. Pretty good house, too."

The two brothers awakened at the cannon shot, with a terrible start, to see as in a nightmare the masked figure of a man sail out from the gun muzzle high, high, in the tent and plummet down in a somersault into a net. There was a burst of applause, and then on all sides the spectators stood up. The audience began to go home.

Since there was no more to the show, the Campbell boys also went home.

With
Laughter

With Laughter

Tom Fennel snapped his fingers, sat up on the divan, and burst into rumbling laughter. "Connie," he said to his wife, "I just realized that all evening I've been trying to put a jinx on you."

His wife interrupted her pacing to gaze at him with amusement. "How come?"

"We agreed we wanted a girl, but I've been a liar. I want another ball-player in the family; I haven't got

"With Laughter" was first published in 1960.

any use for a little old female with ribbons in her hair."

"Then I'll tell you something, pal — if it *is* a girl, don't you try making a tomboy out of her. I — " Connie paused, pressed a hand to the small of her back, then glanced at her wristwatch.

"You have one?" he asked.

"Yes — seven minutes."

"You certainly didn't stay long at eight."

"I'm advancing at a trot," she answered with a pleased smile. "You heard what Jake said — nature built me to whelp easy."

Tom stood up, frowning a little. "How about we call him again?"

"Not yet."

"Why not? You keep saying there's a definite rhythm — "

"Jake's like any doctor. He wants me to have some solid contractions before he decides it's the real thing. So far there's only been these biddy cramps in the back."

"Then why are *you* sure it isn't false labor?"

"Because of the way I feel."

"Can't you tell Jake about it?"

"He's never had a baby, he wouldn't consider my ideas to be medically important."

"And your ideas are what?"

"I told you when you came home — that cow-like feeling I've had these last two months has gone. I feel so alive I could fly. I think it's nature's way of telling a woman her time has come."

Tom laughed. "Sounds like Voodoo talk to me."

He took her face between his hands, kissed her, and said, "You're just working a racket to get attention."

"Okay, go to bed. But don't be surprised if I wake you about three in the morning."

"I'll give you half an hour. Meanwhile I'll go drink a beer to your perfect pelvis."

"It's time you did. You don't appreciate my anatomy enough."

"Yes?" he asked, and burst out laughing.

"And get me a glass of grapefruit juice, will you?"

Tom nodded and raised his voice as he went into the kitchen. "Say, I forgot to tell you about Paulie. When I was taking him over to your ma — "

"Nature calling," his wife interrupted. "Hold it."

"Sure."

Tom returned to the living room with a glass of juice and a beer bottle. He lit a small cigar, drank some of the beer, and crossed to the television set. Then, rather abruptly, he strode into the hallway calling, "What did you say?"

The excitement in Connie's voice was unmistakable. "You can telephone Jake and tell him he guessed wrong. I've had a real contraction."

"You don't say — good for you!" With some haste he dialed their doctor's number. When the elderly voice replied, he said quickly, "Jake? This is Tom Fennell. Connie says she's had a real contraction."

"Ask her where."

Tom called out the question, got the answer, and said quickly, "It was low, in front."

"I guess she's starting."

"The rhythm's down to seven minutes now. Isn't it time she went to the hospital?"

"Yes. You get along and I'll meet you there. And listen, Tom. . . . "

"Yes?"

"Please don't be one of those jerks who get all fussed. Connie's healthy, and the baby's in the right position with its head engaged. So just relax now and help her relax, will you?"

"Sure."

"Okay. See you in about an hour."

"Connie," Tom called, "Jake says it's time to go. I'm calling Walt."

"Take it easy, you'll wake up the neighbors," Connie remarked with amusement as she returned to the living room. "There's no rush."

Tom dialed, shifted from foot to foot while he waited for a response, and then spoke more loudly than he realized. "Hey, Walt, this is Tom. The baby's on the way."

"Good deal," his friend replied. "I'll be over in about fifteen minutes."

"Can't you make it sooner?"

"Man, you haven't called me since ten o'clock, so I just went to bed. I have to get dressed."

"Hop on it, huh?"

Tom hung up and said excitedly, "Is your suitcase ready?"

"All packed."

"What do we do now?"

Connie burst out laughing. "Go finish your beer."

Tom grinned, kissed her, and said, "You're wonderful, Sugar. Say — what did Jake mean when he told me the baby's head was engaged?"

"It means the cutie has moved down low so its head is between the bones of my pelvis . . . right here. It's the normal position for birth. Honey, it's a warm night — why don't we go down and wait for Walt outside?"

"Okay, fine. I'll get your suitcase."

As they started down the stairs he asked, "Was that last one seven minutes?"

"I'm still moving at a trot. We're down to six."

His face furrowed. "That Walt better come on time or I'll break his neck."

"He'll come, Walt's dependable. Don't start worrying, honey, there'll be hours of this yet." They stepped out on the quiet street, and Connie took a deep breath. "Isn't it a beautiful night? I love it out here. It's like living in the country."

The spring moon was high, the night was very still, and it did seem more like a village street than part of a large city. Theirs was a new suburb of modest, two-family homes with an amplitude of old oak trees and green lawns. At this hour most of the residents were in bed, front windows were dark, and the moon, unobscured by tall buildings, was flooding their side of the street with a clean, blue-white light.

"Let's walk, it's good for me," Connie said. "We can leave the suitcase."

"You want your coat on?"

"I'm comfortable." She laughed as she took his

arm. "But I'll sweat plenty in the delivery room, you can count on that."

He asked with curiosity, "Would you like it if I could be there with you?"

"I guess so. At the start, anyway. After that I wouldn't know you were there."

"What do you mean?"

She smiled. "Honey, when a woman is actually giving birth, her whole being is so concentrated on her own feeling — and on that terrific act of pushing out a mountain from inside her — that she wouldn't know if she was alone, or in Yankee Stadium with a hundred thousand people watching. She wouldn't care, either."

They walked in silence for a few minutes. Connie was thinking that elsewhere in the world other women were setting out with their husbands on the same errand of birth, and it gave her a sense of kinship that was strangely warming. And Tom was thinking, "If it's a little old gal, I sure hope she's honey brown like Connie and got her straight hair. It wouldn't be kind if she took after me."

"You know," he said . . .

Abruptly Connie's hand gripped his arm with a power that startled him. Her body had gone rigid, her jaws were clenched, and her eyes had opened so wide that her eyeballs gleamed unnaturally in the moonlight. He felt shaken to the roots. "Darling," he cried, but there was no response. She stood immobile. Then, after half a minute had passed, her rigidity dissolved in a heavy sigh. "Let's get the time," she said with a faint

smile. She took a handkerchief from her pocket and
began wiping her face and neck.

For a moment Tom was unable to make his cigarette-lighter work. Then he blurted out, "Twelve twenty-
four. My God, is that what the real pains are like?"

"That's them, honey. That was a beauty. The
little lady is in a hurry. We've skipped to five minutes."

"What?" he asked with dismay. And then, with
anxiety and anger, "Where's that Walt? Did he stop
for a beer?"

"Now relax. I had Paulie quicker than most
women have a first baby, but I was four hours from
the time of my first contraction."

"All right," he muttered, "but I'd sure like to see
you and your perfect pelvis in the hospital. You're
not trotting any longer, you're starting to gallop."

"Let's walk back. I want to put my coat on."

They waited in silence for another few minutes,
and then Tom exclaimed, "There he is, I know the
motor." He pressed Connie's hand and grinned with
relief. Presently a Buick convertible swung around the
corner and came up to them.

"Walt," Tom called as he picked up the suitcase,
"don't get out, there's no time."

"Okay, shove that in here," their friend replied.

He was an undersized, slender man, with a sharp-
featured, coffee brown face, and with a sly grin always
twitching at the corner of his mouth. He and Tom
had been fast friends since high school. "How you doing, Connie?" he called as he set the suitcase on the
front seat.

Tom opened the rear door of the car, and Connie stepped inside. "I'm fine, thanks so much for coming."

"You gotten bigger since last week. You want to lay a little bet on twins?"

Connie didn't reply. In the act of sitting down she had gripped the front seat with both hands.

"What's the matter?" Tom called from behind her and then stepped in quickly. He put an arm around her for support and covered one of her hands with his. He could feel the hot perspiration on her hand, and the rigidity of her body, and he groaned with sympathy and helplessness. A heavy sigh came then from Connie, her body relaxed, and he helped her back in the seat. "Get going," he said urgently to his friend. "Keep it smooth, huh?"

Connie's head was back on the seat and her eyes were closed. She asked softly, "Did you time it?"

"Damn it, no!" Quickly he reached for his cigarette-lighter.

"From the time the last one ended till this one began," she added. She began to wipe her face.

He studied the dial. "I can't be positive, but I'm almost sure it was five minutes again. Perhaps a shade under."

She opened her eyes and smiled at him. "Good." Then she took his hands in both of hers. "Tom, you're making too much of this. That was a healthy contraction, all right, but it's not as bad as it looks to you. I can take it — nothing's going to happen to me."

"Well," he answered in an effort at lightness, "I was way the hell off in Korea when you had Paulie.

I'm inexperienced. Don't mind if I get a little flustered."

"You look as though you're sitting on nails. I'm just another woman having a baby."

"I love you so much," he muttered, "so much you don't know."

"I do know," she whispered, "and that's what makes this good and exciting, even if there is some pain."

"Hey, how am I driving?" Walt called.

"Perfect," Connie told him. "Just try and avoid any sudden stops, won't you?"

When the next contraction came, Connie muttered, "Oh!" and bent forward under the force of it. It required an act of will for Tom to turn from her face to his watch. For a moment he felt bewildered; then, as he checked the minute hand, he became momentarily unstrung. He checked again.

Connie sat erect. She was panting a little and her lids were half closed over her dark eyes.

"Connie," he muttered apprehensively, "that was only three minutes."

Her eyes opened. "You sure?"

"Yes!"

"It did seem shorter." And then, with keen distress, "Oh, Lord, don't tell me I'm going to have one of those taxicab babies?"

"Will it hurt you if we drive faster?"

"We better."

"Walt . . ."

"Right, I heard you," their friend replied. They

were still on the outskirts of the city, and he pushed the speedometer to sixty. "Connie, is there any way to know how much time you actually have?"

"I'll know better when I get the next one." She was sitting tensely.

"What'll we do . . . I mean . . . we've still got twenty-five, thirty minutes."

"Maybe you can pick up a motorcycle cop," Tom said excitedly. "If a cop'd lead the way, we could go through lights. We'd make it in half that time."

"I'll keep my eye peeled."

Tom turned to his wife with naked anxiety. "What *will* we do if we can't make the hospital?"

For a moment Connie didn't reply. She felt such loss of equilibrium that she couldn't think. It was too shocking to accept — that she might be caught without assistance. Yet now it was a real possibility, and quite terrifying. Without forming her thoughts consciously, she suddenly answered the question with blunt harshness: "We'll have to let nature take its course; we'll stop the car and I'll have it!"

"Without a doctor?"

"*You'll* be the doctor!"

"Look out for that truck!" Tom yelled. "He's turning in."

"I see him," Walt answered, braking the car. "Take it easy, Chum. There won't be any accidents tonight."

"What do you mean about me being the doctor? How can I . . . ?"

"You can do what's necessary!" Connie told him

with determination. "If we get into that spot, you're the midwife."

"What do I do?"

She put her hands on his. "I'll tell you, honey — all I know, anyway. But Tom, listen — I'll really be in a bad way if you don't keep calm. If you realize you *can* help me, you won't get so nervous that you can't."

Tom's big body tightened and his rugged face became very stern. "Okay, Sugar. Don't worry. Just tell me."

"We're making good time," Walt called. "I figure less than twenty-five minutes at this rate."

"Fine," Tom replied quickly, "but don't talk now. Connie has to brief me in case we don't make the hospital."

"We'll just have to hope there are no complications," Connie said tensely. She glanced quickly around the interior of the car. "Oh, Lord, there just isn't enough room in here. I'll need to hold onto something with both hands . . . and if you're going to help me . . . I don't know . . . maybe we can stop by a house where the people are decent . . . Well, we'll just have to face that wherever we stop . . . "

"How much time will we have? Will you have any warning?"

"I'll know in advance, there'll be time."

A contraction interrupted them. Tom flicked his lighter, fixed the time, and waited with set jaws until Connie opened her eyes.

"Three minutes again."

She nodded and sighed and then smiled at him as she wiped her face. "I'm doing fine. It's like having an old-fashioned bellyache — nothing a person can't take. This handkerchief is soaked. Open the suitcase and pull out a diaper, will you? I'll baptise it for the baby."

He did so, hands and body moving very fast. Then he said urgently, "Get back to making me a midwife."

"Well . . . let's see . . . " she chuckled ruefully . . . "it's six years since I took that class for pregnant women. Well . . . I guess there's nothing at all you can do until the baby's head begins to be born. Just wait, and if I make some loud noises, don't think there's anything wrong. It's a woman's privilege to yell a little."

He pressed her hand. "Go on."

"Here's one thing I remember well, Tom. When enough of the head is in the clear so that you can take hold of it, you have to support it with a hand on either side." She gestured, "Like this."

"Okay."

"And what you do, honey, is to *lift* the head *gently*. In that way you help the head get born and it makes it easier on me."

"All right, I'm clear on that."

"What next?" she wondered aloud. "Oh, yes . . . listen . . . when the baby's head appears, its face is turned down. But once the head is born, it'll start to turn up. Don't interfere with that."

"Go on."

They hit a rough spot in the pavement then, and the car jounced heavily. Walt called back, "Sorry," and Connie said, "no harm done."

"We're in the city anyway," Tom muttered. "What else?"

"I'm thinking . . . Well . . . when the head is all born, the hard part for *me* is over. But you'll have to watch out then because the body'll come out quickly — it sort of slides out, Tom, like those kittens we saw." She stopped talking as the car slowed down for a red light. Walt looked to both sides, saw no cars, and stepped on the gas without waiting for the light to change. "What else?" Connie continued, "I must be forgetting . . . "

A contraction began and her hand, which had been on Tom's knee, tightened like a clamp. "Oh, Lord," she whispered heavily when it was over, "that one surely paralyzed me; it was fierce."

"Still three minutes," he told her.

Connie wiped her forehead and neck with the diaper. She said wanly, "Starting to sweat good."

"What do I do after the baby is born? I have to hold it upside down and slap it, don't I?"

"Wait," she whispered. She put her head back against the seat. Presently, with closed eyes, she began to talk again. "Yes, hold it upside down, but if it cries by itself, you don't need to slap it." She mopped her forehead. "Seems to me I must be skipping things you ought to know, darn it. Here's something . . . when the baby is fully born, you'll absolutely need your two hands to hold it. That's very important."

"Okay." He was wondering how so many thoughts, images, fears, could be racing through his brain at the same time that his whole being was concentrated upon her instructions.

She opened her eyes and smiled at him. "And remember, a newborn baby is as slippery and wriggly as anything. I guess that's why a doctor always gets a grip on the ankles."

"Sounds like nothing at all," he told her in an effort to relieve his tremendous tension. "Catching a football on the run is much harder. Have I graduated? Is that all I have to know?"

"A baby gets born in three stages," she reminded him in a controlled way, but with fatigue showing. "That's only the second."

"Oh, God, yes! But how can I cut the cord?"

"Well . . . guess you won't be able to. Wrap the baby up and keep it warm. Let Walt find the way to call an ambulance."

"Will you be all right like that . . . and the baby?"

"Yes. Just let Walt be sure to describe the situation. Then the ambulance can come prepared."

"Walt, did you hear that?" Tom called.

"No."

Tom repeated it.

"Okay, but we ought to be there in almost fifteen minutes now."

A low groan burst from Connie's lips and Tom, without looking at his watch, knew that the rhythm had changed again. Under the lighter he saw that it was a fraction over two minutes. When he could speak to Connie again and had told her, she nodded, panting, and then whispered, "Tell Walt — I'm afraid we haven't got fifteen minutes."

"Are you sure? You feel that way?"

She nodded.

"Walt," he called urgently, "Connie doesn't think there's time."

"You want me to stop?"

Tom turned to his wife. "Not just yet," he called back, "but get ready."

"God Almighty!" Walt shouted excitedly, "what am I being so dumb about? There's a hospital on Franklin Avenue, it's only a few blocks." He slowed to take a corner. "We're going there."

"Do you know anything about it?"

"It's small — a denominational hospital. I pass it on my way to work."

"But do you know anything about it?"

"Don't know and don't care," Walt answered as he swung around a second corner, picked up speed, and started back in the direction from which they had come. "This is an emergency, isn't it? We're there in a minute."

"Connie?" Tom asked, peering at her. "All right?"

"So far." She grasped his hand in both of hers. "Oh, I hope there's no trouble!"

Tom didn't answer. He was stroking her arm.

"There it is," Walt shouted. He was slowing down. "I'll run into the office and alert them. You bring Connie."

It was a rather new brick building, three stories

in height. Most of the windows were dark, but the entrance was lighted, and there were lights in one section of the ground floor, presumably the offices. It looked like the type of private institution in which there might be good equipment and service, even though there were only twenty or thirty beds.

The car stopped. Walt leaped out and ran for the steps.

"All right to walk?" Tom asked urgently.

"Yes."

He helped her out, both hands grasping her arms, and Connie said quietly, "I'm not counting on it, honey, I'm counting on *you*." She gave a low grunt and her hands seized his arms. Her head fell forward.

"Oh, sweetheart, darling," he muttered. The weight of her head was on his chest, and he had a wild hunger to fling his arms around her and comfort her with his kisses, and at the same time he thought that he ought to be checking the interval since the last contraction — but he did nothing because her hands were like clamps upon his arms and he dared not move.

"Oh, my!" Connie sighed. She was panting, her head still resting on his chest. "It won't be long now." With effort she straightened up. "Let's go."

"I didn't get the time."

"Never mind." She was breathing heavily, obviously needing the support of his arm around her.

"Can you manage the steps? You want me to carry you?

"No . . . but go slow."

They were only on the second step when they

heard loud voices from the other side of the entrance
door, which had been left slightly ajar. Connie stopped
abruptly. The door opened and they saw Walt, gesti-
culating, talking intensely — and opposite him a tall,
lean, white man of thirty-five who was standing with
his legs wide apart and his hands on his hips. "But my
God," Walter was crying rather incoherently, "he's a
war veteran, how can you let a pregnant woman . . .?"

"I told you already — there's no doctor on duty,"
the other man interrupted uncomfortably.

"There are nurses, you . . ."

"This hospital has a policy, and I'm not going to
be the one to violate it."

A middle-aged nurse suddenly appeared behind
them. She cried out, "But, Mr. Clark, this is an emergency, it won't affect . . ."

"Don't interfere," Clark interrupted with resentment. "And don't tell me how to lose my job. I'm
Night Supervisor, not you. I'm the one the Board'll hold
responsible, not you."

Stunned, knowing the whole of it already while
still unable to accept it, and feeling as though he were
strangling, Tom cried out, "Are you saying my wife
can't come in?"

"This hospital doesn't accept colored patients."

A bull roar burst from Tom's throat and he let go
of Connie. "The hell you say, you son of a bitch.
We haven't got time. She's going in and you won't
stop it!"

"You try to force your way in, and you'll be committing an illegal act," Clark replied without moving. "In my desk drawer I've got a pistol and a license to use it. Don't make me."

"Tom," Connie cried, *"please, please."* She caught his coat. "Take me back to the car."

He turned to her, putting his arm around her, his face contorted with rage, his mouth open and working. He wanted to beat this man to a pulp, to force their way in — but Connie's cry had cut through everything. There was no time for trial or error, and her voice had told him that. It was Walt who spoke out what was useless: "You think this'll read good in the newspapers? You think you still can treat us like cattle and get away with it? You stony-hearted bastard, I'll see that it gets out!"

For the first time Clark lost his composure. "Let it!" he snapped with passion. He eyes blazed and he began to tremble with indignation. "Where do you get off insulting me? Nobody asked you here: This hospital was built by white folks for their private use. You've pushed your way into the schools and movies and restaurants of this city, but you won't get in here. Go to your own hospital. Go have your nigger babies in the damn Supreme Court."

"Oh, — look!" the middle-aged nurse cried distractedly from the doorway, "look at her."

The Fennells had taken only a few steps toward the car when Connie had stopped abruptly. With the awareness of a swimmer who is half-drowned, yet still can clutch at a piece of wood in the water, she had turned back. In front of the hospital there was an iron fence and her hands were reaching out for it blindly. Her body was sinking into the ancient, primitive squat of a woman in labor.

"Oh!" the nurse cried, "she's having it now!" She disappeared inside.

Connie's hands, one of them still holding the diaper, found the rods of the fence. A grunt sounded deep in her throat, her body jerked forward, and then, as she strained and bore down, a low cry issued from her lips.

Walt ran over to Tom, his face twisted with rage, "What can I do?"

Tom, with one arm supporting his wife, did not hear. He was fixed upon her, and he looked frantic. After half a minute the contraction stopped, but Connie did not let go of the railing. Her head was almost touching the bars, and she was panting heavily. She sank back suddenly, exhausted, the full weight of her body upon his arm. Her eyes were closed. In the spill of light from the hospital doorway Tom could see the hot blood flush under her skin, and the running sweat on her face. He cried frantically, "Connie, let me get you to the car."

Her eyes opened and she seemed to be having difficulty in focussing on his face.

"Let me get you to the car!"

"No," she whispered tiredly, yet with a self-possession that astonished him, "don't move me, darling. The baby's coming now."

"Oh, not here!" he cried out involuntarily, "not on the street!"

In reply Connie gasped deeply for air. Then her body jerked forward, her hands seizing the railing again. A low, moaning grunt burst from her lips, and she bore down with the contraction.

"Let *me* hold her," Walt cried. *"You* have to help the birth."

Tom didn't reply. He was staring at his wife with anguish and desolation.

The middle-aged nurse ran out of the doorway. "I called an ambulance." Abruptly, with a small, meaningless cry, she ran back inside.

Connie sank back heavily on Tom's arm. She spoke with effort, as though she were half asleep. "Help me lie down." Then, as Tom lowered her to the sidewalk, she seemed to awaken. "Oh! — there are so many things I forgot to tell you."

"About the . . ." Her words turned into a gasp for air. She seized Walt's arms, and a low groan burst from her open mouth.

"Oh, Christ!" Tom cried, sobbing aloud. "Here on the street!" He dropped to his knees, his whole being sour with fear. His heart was hammering against the wall of his chest, and he told himself that he could not give his wife the help she needed, that something would go wrong and she would die, that his shaking hands never could hold a baby, that he had forgotten everything.

"Tom?" Her voice came weakly. "Tom?" He saw the look on her strained, beloved face, and her aching need rose like fire within him, and he cried out to her in a clotted voice, "Yes, I'm here, I'll take care of you."

He became one with her then. The world blotted out. There was only Connie and himself and their child to be given life. He was not aware when a passing auto stopped and two white men got out of it to stand on the sidewalk and gape — nor did he hear Walt speak to them so savagely that they left. He did not see a light go on in one of the upstairs rooms of the hospital, or hear a window being open, or hear voices saying, "What's going on down there? *What?* Hey — that woman's having a baby!"

He heard nothing except the deep grunts and low birth cries of his wife. These possessed him, and it was as though his heart were inside her heart so that he, too, was part of the rhythm of this birth, and the hands with which he would deliver became sure and steady. With fiery calm, he waited for each new contraction, for the moment when he would do for his wife what she needed. The moment came quickly. He heard a succession of low, deep cries from Connie that seemed to echo and re-echo in the hot stillness of his mind — and then he was supporting the tiny, warm head between his hands and lifting it gently as he had been told.

A voice from the outside slipped into his consciousness then, angering him before he even knew what it was saying. He tried to shut it out, but he could not. "Don't bear down till I tell you, dearie. Pant, keep panting, that's the way." He turned to see a nurse — a young, blond, *white* nurse — standing over his wife, and he burst out with a sob, "Get away! We don't need you."

"You certainly do need me," the nurse answered firmly, but without offense. "If the cord's not in the right place, the baby can strangle. Keep panting, dearie." And then, as she leaned over by Tom to inspect the position of the umbilical cord, "You're doing fine, Mister, but pay attention to me . . . Good, everything's fine. Bear down now, dearie. Another minute and it's over."

The head began to rotate with the next contraction, and, with that wondrous motion of birth, jubilation rose like a sweet sap within Tom's heart. The right shoulder appeared, and then the left, and he didn't hear his own cry when finally the tiny, exquisite body was lying on his arm, and the warm, tiny ankles were between his fingers.

"Oh, wonderful, everything's grand!" the nurse said with delight. "Now keep holding the ankles, Mister, and turn him upside down. He has to spit out before he can breathe. Oh, fine!"

The newborn cry sounded, and the new life wriggled and began to move its arms, and Tom didn't know that he was weeping. "My wife," he cried, "is she all right?"

"Why wouldn't she be? An easy birth if I ever saw one. Here — wrap the little fellow in this — we have to keep him warm." She glanced over at Walt, who still was kneeling behind Connie, unable to realize that his services no longer were needed. He looked exhausted. "Hey, Mister, you — I dropped a sheet and blanket somewhere — there they are. She needs to be covered. Put the sheet under her."

"The cord," Tom said with excitement. "How — ?"

"Came down all prepared," the nurse interrupted. She was smiling with a kind of triumph that he could not understand, a thin, blond, attractive girl in her early twenties who was giving the lie to all of the blind rage in his heart. "Got some cord ties," she continued, pulling a sterile package from one of her pockets, "got scissors, got Kelly clamps, that's all we need. I would've been down earlier, but it took time for the news to get to the top floor. It sure was a quick birth. I — "

"But my wife," Tom interrupted with anxiety, "she's so quiet."

"Just sleeping. She's had some hard work, Mister, she'll wake up in a few minutes. Hold the baby nearer to me now. Isn't he a howler! Thinks he owns the world!" Her hands worked deftly. She cut the cord and said to Tom, who had shivered perceptibly, "Everything's normal, don't get worried. Cover him up now. He's ready to sleep a little."

Tom said in a low voice, "Can you take him for a minute? My knees are giving me hell, I need to stand up."

She did so and he stood up slowly, rubbing his knees, and turned slowly toward the hospital steps with his shoulders hunching over and his thick neck swelling. "You would've let my wife die," he cried in a thick voice. "You no-good bastard, you were ready to see her die."

"No, Tom, don't be a fool!" Walt cried. He caught Tom's arm, was shaken off, caught it again. "Listen," he lied, I hear the ambulance coming. There's always a cop with every ambulance."

Tom shook him off — and then suddenly burst into dry, wracked sobs. "Oh, my God, I'm glad I was born black! It's easier to be human." He stumbled toward his wife, crying out to the nurse, "Is she all right, are you sure?"

"Yes — she's waking up now."

"Out on the street!" Tom cried. The tears began running down his face. "She could've died."

A heavy sigh came from Connie and her eyes half opened. Bending over her, the nurse said quickly, "Everything's fine, dearie, the baby and you."

"Tom? Tom?" Connie murmured.

"I'm here." Still sobbing, he kneeled down by her and kissed her cheek and forehead.

"Oh!" she said, and became fully awake. "It's normal? Everything all right?"

"All normal," the nurse told her, "a boy."

A slow smile came to Connie's face. "How nice. Let me see him . . . Oh, what a darling!"

"I hear the ambulance," Walt exclaimed jubilantly, telling the truth this time.

The nurse nodded. "Good. The birth's not over yet, you know." She opened Connie's dress. "Put him to suck. It'll help your contractions."

"Where did *you* come from?" Connie asked with surprise. "Did you deliver me?"

"I only helped. Your husband did the job."

"Oh, Tom, sweet Tom," Connie murmured, "I knew I could count on you." And then, as though her rapture could not be contained, she began to laugh, a tired, soft, joyous laugh that sounded in the night like a clear bell. It was a laughter that spoke of all that was good and healthy and hopeful in life, and it came from her like a bird-song at dawn, and at the hearing of it Clark, the superintendent, entered the hospital and shut the door.

The Farmer's Dog

The Farmer's Dog

    Last year, in London, I went to a dog show with
some friends — Hugh Stuart, a physiologist, and his
wife, Libby. While we were there we met a man named
Edmund Donat. Polish by birth, he was a chemist in
the concern where Libby worked as a stenographer.
When we were leaving at tea time, Libby invited Donat
to join us. He accepted with such shy and manifest
pleasure that it seemed evident he led a rather lonely
life. He was a tall man, a bit stooped, nearly bald, with

"The Farmer's Dog" was first published in 1968.

pleasant features and handsome, dark eyes, but with an unhealthy pallor. He appeared to be about fifty-five and I was surprised to learn later that he was ten years younger. Subsequently Libby told us that he had contracted typhus during World War II when he was a prisoner in a concentration camp, and that he still was suffering neurological difficulties — just what, she didn't know.

When he had ordered tea, Hugh fell to ribbing his wife in an affectionate way about the limited intelligence of dogs. It had become clear as soon as we entered the show that Libby was a fervent dog-lover and Hugh had tagged along reluctantly in a spirit of marital compromise. Whenever she expressed enchantment with a dog, he would mutter: "I've dissected the breed, darling — its brain is the size of a pea," — or, "inbred for generations; has a wretched nervous system." Libby hadn't seemed to mind his remarks, although occasionally she would poke him with her elbow and say, "Shut up, fish-lover"; and she regarded him now with a tolerant smile as he continued to needle her. Presently she said to Donat with a bubbling laugh, "You see what I'm married to? He doesn't like dogs because they're not something else." And, to her husband, "You idiot, can you herd sheep like a collie? I like a dog for what he is — even though you say an octopus is more intelligent."

"An octopus reasons, my dear, and uses a tool to open the clam he wants to eat. Dogs can be taught certain things, but they don't reason."

"If I may comment," Donat put in, "I believe there is a wide range in the intelligence of dogs just as there is in the human being. At the upper level there surely are some dogs that *are* capable of intelligent reasoning."

"Have you concrete evidence of that?" Hugh asked.

"I think so."

"What?"

"I once saw a dog in a fearful predicament. I believe she reasoned about what was best to do. But I can't give you the evidence in a few words."

"We're in no hurry. Please tell us."

Donat gazed at each of us in turn as though to make certain we really wanted to hear him out. When Libby said eagerly, "Do tell us, please," he nodded, smiled in a shy way, and began. He had a marked accent, but his English was fluent.

"The name of the dog was Pani — that means 'Madame' or 'Mrs.' in Polish. But I must explain first that when Germany invaded Poland in thirty-nine, I was living in Warsaw. My father sent my mother and me to a farm he owned about thirty miles away. We never saw him again, he was called up to the army and killed, but that's another matter . . .

"There was a house on the farm where we used to spend our holidays. The land, about ten acres, was worked by a tenant family and I was a good friend of the two sons. One of them was my age, almost seventeen, and the other, Antek, was a year older. Pani obeyed everyone in the family, but above all she was

Antek's dog. Between Pani and Antek there was an understanding, and there was a love, that were quite extraordinary."

Until this point in his narrative Donat had been talking in a matter of fact way. However, when he referred to the bond between his friend and the dog, his eyes began to kindle, and from then on his face gradually became more and more animated.

"In December, 1939, when the Germans had all of Poland under their control, they issued an order that every thoroughbred of certain breeds — Great Dane, Doberman pinscher, German shepherd, and a few others — was to be turned over to them. All other dogs were to be destroyed."

"Why destroyed?" Libby asked stiffly.

"Why not?" Donat answered with a smile. "It was a logical decision by an Army Command waging a ruthless war. They needed certain dogs for guard duty; all others were to them useless consumers of food. In fact they regarded people more or less the same way. Well, so immediately Antek heard of it, he hid Pani in the barn. He did more than lock her in — he built a hiding place under the floor that would have been hard to find. He would take her out for exercise at night, and visit her several times during the day."

"Didn't the dog bark?" Hugh asked.

"Oh, no, not even when Antek entered the barn."

"Because he muzzled her?"

"No, because he told her not to bark."

Hugh raised his eyebrows and Donat, observing it, smiled a little, but offered no explanation.

"About a week later, early in the morning, an army truck came to the farm. There were three S.S. men in their black uniforms and, with them, a Polish interpreter, a turncoat from one of the border regions. Inside the truck there were two dogs chained to the sideboards. Well, the whole family was there and the interpreter, an arrogant little weasel, said to the father, 'Where are your dogs?' It was young Antek who answered him: 'We only had one dog and it died several weeks ago.' At this the weasel burst out laughing. He said, 'There's been a regular plague in this district — so many dogs have died recently.' "

Donat paused, ran a hand over his head, and muttered, "You hate an enemy, but a turncoat makes you burn with special rage. Anyway, this weasel translated into German and the corporal in charge snapped an order. Then that one, the corporal, walked up to Antek and aimed a pistol at his face. Antek's mother let out a scream and ran toward them, but one of the S.S. stopped her with such a shove that she fell down. The rest of us stood where we were, paralyzed." Donat swallowed, and again ran a hand over his head. "The weasel said to Antek, 'I'll count ten. If you don't say where the dog is in that time, the German will kill you, and don't think he won't.' Well, before he even began to count, the mother screamed out from the ground, 'The dog's in the barn.' "

Again Donat paused, then spoke very softly. "I'll never forget the look Antek gave his mother — as though it was him she'd betrayed. It was a moment to freeze the soul."

At this point Hugh asked with keen interest, "Do you think Antek would have kept silent?"

"I don't know. When I asked him later, he told me honestly that *he* didn't know. But my feeling at the time was that the dog was as precious to him as anyone in the family, and he would not have spoken. Anyway, after the mother told, the weasel let out a guffaw and said, 'How clever you peasants are! Your dead dogs are always alive in the barn.' Well, so the father was sent to bring Pani out."

"*Was* she a thoroughbred?" Libby asked.

Donat shook his head. "A mongrel. We were certain the Germans would shoot her. Antek, naturally, was frantic. He began to plead with the interpreter, to tell him what a wonderful dog Pani was, to beg him to take her even though she was not a hundred-percent thoroughbred. He was carrying on awful, sobbing and half incoherent. His manner aroused the curiosity of the Germans because they asked the weasel to translate. Well, presently Pani came into view. How shall I describe her? She was a big dog, larger than a German shepherd, with a tremendous chest, and with the muzzle and jaws of a Great Dane. She had short, brown hair, a bushy tail, and a wide black ring around her neck. We used to speculate about her bloodline. We knew nothing about her, you see. Antek had found her, a stray puppy. It was clear she had many strains in her — as though a larger Boxer had mated with a Labrador retriever, and their issue with a German shepherd, and down the line a Dane or even a mastiff. From all of this crossbreeding had come a dog that seemed to have inherited only the best from each of its sires. There was so much alertness in the way she looked at you, so much intelligence in her brown eyes, so much power and self-possession in the way she walked, that one almost could say she looked regal. There was no doubt the Germans were impressed with her. Antek, of course, never let up pleading. Through the interpreter he begged the corporal to show Pani to his superiors. He promised by all the Saints that she'd learn whatever they wanted quicker than any other dog, and that she would be obedient to the death. Well, finally, that was how the corporal decided it. They took Pani away."

Hugh asked, "Did the dog fight to keep off the truck?"

"No, because Antek himself jumped on it and called her. He told the corporal she wouldn't need to be muzzled or chained like the others, but he insisted, and Antek did it. Then he put his arms around Pani and spoke to her a moment. He came down blubbering like a child."

Libby asked, "Was an arrangement made so Antek would be told what they did with Pani?"

Donat smiled. "Conquerors don't make arrangements. So far as Antek knew, it was farewell one way or another."

Hugh said, "But I judge it wasn't farewell?"

"No. Five months later we met Pani again. It came about because Antek, his brother, and I, joined an illegal Resistance group. Antek and I were arrested one night, when we were on a mission, because it was after the curfew hour and we had no pass. We were a month in prison in Warsaw, and then we were shipped to the concentration camp of Auschwitz. Fortunately for us, we were only there a few days, very fortunately. Together we were sent to a labor camp where there were about a thousand men. The work we had was to build a road from a new airfield to a main highway. It was killing labor, dawn to dark seven days a week, and the food was miserable and insufficient, but if a man was strong to begin with, he could survive — provided he had luck. By luck, I mean that he didn't get sick or hurt so he'd be shipped back to Auschwitz. We did have one blessed privilege: We were allowed to wash in some swamp water twice a week so we could keep free of lice. Well, so Pani wasn't at the camp when we arrived — at least we never noticed her. But one morning in June Antek saw her with another work Commando."

Donat paused, ran a hand over his head as he seemed to do every time he felt special emotion, and there was a slight hoarseness in his voice as he went on. "I wish I could describe to you how Antek behaved that night. I myself didn't see Pani, and although Antek and I were in the same Commando, we couldn't speak at work. It was not until we were in the barrack that he could tell me. He came up to me like a man who had just buried his child. His eyes and face were wild. He said, 'Pani's here and she doesn't remember me!' Well, after some questions, I got an account from him. But first you must understand something important about our conditions there: Every work Commando had about forty men and was guarded by two Capos, two S.S.

men, and three dogs. A Capo was a prisoner who carried a club and acted as an overseer, and who got
special food and privileges for the filthy work he did.
Usually they were men with a criminal background,
brutes who had lost their humanity. But in spite of
them, and the S.S. guards with their rifles and tommy-
guns, it would not have been impossible for determined
men to sometimes escape. Some would have been killed
or caught, but others would have gotten away, and
many of us were desperate enough to try. It was the
dogs that prevented us. You have no idea how those
dogs had been trained to ferocity toward us prisoners.
All of us looked the same, by the way, the same striped
clothes, the same shaven heads. At every work site one
dog remained with an S.S. man, and the other two
guarded the perimeters — that is, the outside line permitted us. If a man came within ten feet of the line,
the dog on that side would be on its feet with a snarl
that would curdle your blood, and also would alert the
guards. At five feet, without warning, the dog would
attack with an absolutely insane fury. In only our
second week there, during a rain, a man slipped in the
mud and rolled down an embankment over the line.
By the time a guard ran up, he was dead, his face un-
recognizable, his throat mangled. It didn't take more
than that to make us all tremble before those horrible
dogs. We knew that even if we bolted into the woods
without getting shot, those dogs would be at our throats
sooner or later. Well . . . this explains to you why Antek
was so heartsick. That morning, when our Commando
was being counted, he was standing in an outside file.

Another Commando moved up alongside ours. He saw Pani not two yards from him — a guard had her on a chain leash. Naturally he didn't dare call to her. What stunned him then was to see Pani suddenly turn her head and look at him. He said she gazed at him steadily for about thirty seconds, but without any sign of recognition, just staring at him the way a man might. Then her Commando moved off. Yet, as Antek said, Pani was a dog, not a man, and unless she had forgotten him completely, it was impossible she wouldn't react to him."

"And she had forgotten him?" Libby asked intently. "I don't see why. An intelligent dog shouldn't forget its master in only five months."

"Wait, you'll hear," said Donat. "What troubled Antek most was the thought that the S.S. had transformed his beloved Pani into the same kind of wild beast the other dogs were. 'I would have preferred her dead,' he said to me. 'I didn't dream they would do this to her.' I remember what I answered him. I meant it to be a comfort, but it wasn't. I said, 'if they can turn a schoolboy into a murdering S.S. man, why isn't it easier with a dog?' All Antek did was look at me and walk away . . . Well, about a week later our Commando had a change of guards. With one of the new S.S. came Pani. The first time I saw her assigned to a perimeter of our work site, I feared her and hated her like any other dog. And yet it struck me by the second day that there was something strange in her behavior. Because each time Antek's work brought him anywhere in her view, I had the feeling she was quietly watching him."

Hugh said, "Are you telling us that she *had* recognized Antek, but was not letting on? That's hard to believe."

"Antek noticed the same thing and neither of us knew what to believe."

"How did Pani act with you?" Libby asked.

"It happens I rarely was close to her, either on the march or at work. Once, when I did come close, she looked at me exactly as she had at Antek the first time. I didn't know what to make of it."

"And how did she act with the other prisoners?" Libby asked.

"Like the other dogs."

"Did she ever attack one of them?"

"I'll tell you about that in a moment. Well, so after a week of this Antek said to me one morning, 'I didn't sleep last night. I'm convinced Pani *does* know me. I'm going to find out.' I asked him how. He said he didn't know — he would think of a way. Two days later he made an opportunity. It was after our midday meal — the bread and some of that lovely nettle soup they gave us day after day. When the whistle blew, Antek jumped quickly and picked up his wheelbarrow. As he passed Pani, he tipped it over — it was a load of sand. Then he ran for a shovel, meanwhile getting a kick for his clumsiness from a Capo. Well, I was in a position to watch him shoveling up the sand, and to watch Pani also. It was a hot day and she was lying down in the shade of a bush with her big tongue lolling out. The sand had fallen on hard earth about four yards away from her, but some of it spilling closer. As Antek shoveled it, he moved nearer to her. Meanwhile, although I didn't know it until later, he kept saying her name in a low tone. When he reached the danger line, Pani jumped up. And then something astonishing occurred: She didn't snarl at him or get ready to spring, but she looked over at the guard who was *her* guard — and then she turned back to Antek and watched him without making a sound. Immediately that happened, I looked over at the guard also — he was a distance away relieving his boredom by throwing stones at some birds. When I looked back at Pani, Antek had one leg no more than three feet from her. Of course, he was taking the chance of being seen by a Capo or a guard, but with all the work going on he wasn't noticed. And Pani still did nothing, she didn't even snarl at him. Then, when he moved away, she lay down again.

"So, you *are* telling us she knew him, but was concealing it," Hugh said.

"What else?" Libby exclaimed. "It's perfectly clear."

"Not to me."

With a luminous glow in his dark eyes, Donat said, "You'll be able to draw conclusions better in a moment . . . That night Antek was in a fever. He'd gotten an idea and nothing could shake it. Not only was he convinced Pani knew him, like you say, but something more. He swore to us that Pani knew *she* was a prisoner of the Germans just like him. 'I'm forced to build a road for them,' he told us, 'and she's a prisoner forced to do guard duty. But she knows she's a prisoner.' Donat paused, smiled, and shook his head.

"Nothing could convince Antek otherwise. It was not only I who told him that *no* dog could have such logical understanding, but others told him also. There was a group of us who relied on one another, we were good comrades. One was a farm boy like Antek, a second was a young priest, and the third, interestingly enough, was a veterinarian. It was he who insisted more than any of us that Antek was loony on the subject of his dog. 'No,' Antek kept replying, 'I could see it in her eyes. I know what she was telling me.' Well, the next morning Antek called us together again. He said, 'Pani and I are going to escape. I'm telling you so you can be prepared. When I run, it may be a chance for you. I can't tell you when I'll do it. Keep your eyes open.' "

Donat paused for a moment, stroked his head, then sipped some tea. "Our arguments had no effect. We pointed out that even if Pani didn't attack him, the two other dogs would be after him right away. To this Antek answered that he would run with a tool in his hand, and Pani and he could handle them. When the veterinarian begged him to test Pani further, Antek answered that he simply had to seize the first opportunity — perhaps Pani would be changed to another Commando. So that morning, even though I hadn't decided what I would do, I followed Antek's example: I put my ration of bread inside my shirt instead of eating it — Well, an hour after work started, I gave up any idea of escaping. By accident I threw a shovelful of gravel so that a small stone struck a Capo in the leg. He clubbed me so hard across the back that he knocked me down. Then he fell to kicking me. By the time he let up, I knew running away was not possible; it took all my strength and willpower merely to lift my shovel. A little while later something else happened that made me feel sure Antek also would have to give up the idea of escape. One of the prisoners — I learned later he was sick with a high fever, but was trying to hide it — became delirious in the hot sun. With a shovel in his hand he started to walk like a blind man directly toward Pani. She jumped up with a terrible, warning snarl — and at the same moment the man reeled and fainted. What Pani would have done if he had fallen toward her instead of away from her, I can't actually say, although my belief is she would have done what she was trained to do. Anyway, when Antek passed me a moment later, I whispered to him, 'Don't run!' He didn't answer me, his face was like stone — and a few minutes later he ran."

Donat smiled faintly and said in a quiet, tremulous way, "Now I will explain our geography. Our Commando was breaking stone from a hillside to use for the roadbed. We were spread out for maybe seventy-five yards with one S.S. man at the head of the line and the other at the rear. The hillside rose quite steep and was barren, so no dog had been stationed there. On the other side of us, commencing only thirty feet or so away, there was a big field of sunflowers. I think maybe you have not seen such a field. The plants grow seven and eight feet tall before the seeds are ready for harvest. A man can run into a field like that and be lost to view in a second. However, there were two dogs stationed on that side, Pani close by, and a Doberman pinscher about thirty yards ahead. Well, the Capo nearest us ordered two of the prisoners to carry the man who had fainted to one of the trucks we were loading. While his eye was on them. Antek dropped his wheelbarrow. He picked up a crowbar he had put in it beforehand and suddenly he was running at full speed for the shelter of the sunflowers. He was about five yards to one side of Pani and I heard him yell, 'Pani, come!' — that was all, not another word."

"And Pani?" Libby burst out.

"For one moment my blood froze," Donat answered. "Pani bounded up with a terrible snarl. With one tremendous jump she was right at Antek's heel. In the next second I expected her to leap on his back. And then, as though some chain had suddenly pulled her up short, she stopped where she was. I . . ."

"She caught his scent!" Libby interrupted excitedly. "She reacted before knowing it was Antek."

"Yes, I think so," Donat agreed, "but it was more complicated than that. By this time a whole series of things were happening at once. Antek disappeared into that thick forest of plants. At the same time the guard behind us, about thirty yards back, started shooting. He had a submachine gun and he sprayed the area in Antek's direction, he shot off a whole clip, I don't know how many bullets, but many. Meanwhile the guard in front had yelled a command at the Doberman pinscher

near him. That dog ran into the field directly opposite
where he was, and he was followed by a black German
shepherd that the guard had loosed from his chain —
and then that guard himself, with a rifle, ran into the
field. I can't tell you whether all of this happened in
five seconds or ten or thirty — but meanwhile Pani remained where she was, half-crouching, absolutely motionless. I didn't have time for any thoughts then, but
later I felt I understood her behavior — she was paralyzed by opposing forces. Antek had been only partially
right about her. She knew him and wouldn't attack him,
but the discipline of her training under the S.S. prevented her from running with him. She was a prisoner
in a deeper sense than he knew. And it is my belief
that in those few moments that she remained motionless there was a terrible struggle going on in — what?
— her feelings, her soul, her intelligence? I think all of
it, a struggle such as a man would have."

"Oh, come now," said Hugh. "Why attribute . . .?"

"But you haven't heard yet," Donat interrupted
emotionally, "because in the next moment Pani let out
a howl that made me think she had been wounded by
one of the bullets. It wasn't a snarl, or a bark or anything except a kind of wounded howl, as though she
was suffering pain. And in the very next second she
disappeared into the sunflowers." With a nervous gesture
Donat wiped some beads of perspiration from his forehead. "If it is possible for a man to continue living
although his heart has stopped beating, then my heart
stopped when I lost sight of Pani. Was she running to
escape with Antek, or to tear him to pieces with the

other dogs? I didn't know. Everything was confusion, a blur, a nightmare. What direction was Antek taking? The field of sunflowers was perhaps six hundred yards deep. It ran on a decline away from us so that I could see on the other side, where it ended, a pasture with cows, and some farm buildings. In back of the pasture the land rose to a wooded hill. Antek surely would try to go there, I thought. Then, suddenly, from off in the field, there was the most savage howling of dogs. 'They've caught him,' I thought, and I heard myself beginning to scream without my wanting to and without being able to stop. The howling kept up and then there were rifle shots — half-a-dozen, maybe. And then, suddenly, there was the most awful quiet, like the quiet of death. It lasted, that quiet, lasted and lasted until I felt entombed, but later I knew that it could not have been more than two or three minutes. And then I saw Antek."

Donat's dark eyes were glowing luminously. He seemed almost unaware of our presence as he relived the moment of seeing Antek alive. "I saw him running near the farm buildings. Everyone saw him, including the S.S. man who had remained behind. But he couldn't do anything because his submachine gun had no effect at that distance. Antek ran behind a barn and, when we next saw him, he was climbing the hill toward the trees. I didn't actually see him enter the trees because right then happened a tragedy. My two other comrades, the veterinarian and the priest, had not run. But suddenly now — what made him do it? — the young priest bolted for the field. It was madness. The S.S. man had

stationed himself so he could command the area between us and the field. He cut our friend to pieces."

There was a moment's silence. Then Libby asked,
"And Pani? Was she with Antek?"

"No. Presently out of the field came the other S.S.
man. His left arm was bloody and the front of his uniform was ripped open. Hobbling by his side was the
black shepherd; one of its forelegs was dangling, bloody
and bitten through. I didn't know German, but there
were others who did. They made out what the guard
yelled — that Pani — he called her by a German name
— had gone insane — ripped open the throat of the
pinscher, crippled the shepherd, and then, when the
S.S. man came upon them, attacked him also. He had
shot her."

"Ah," Libby exclaimed, "it's what you said when
you began. In a most terrible predicament . . ." She
didn't finish, but turned to her husband and murmured,
"No flip comments, please. I'm not in the mood."

"I don't feel flip," Hugh said quietly. "I'll admit
to being impressed. By any chance, do you know what
happened to Antek?"

"Yes, I do. He made his way to a group of partisans. He survived the war, and he's a farmer again.
Occasionally we write."

The Cop

The Cop

Before he lost his legs Enzo must have been an impressive man, one of those six-foot, burly Italians of the north. He was about fifty when I met him, still handsome in a craggy way, with only a sprinkling of white in his black hair. He always sat dominatingly erect in his wheelchair, his powerful hands on the stumps of his thighs, a lusty glint in his dark eyes. The trattoria he owned, which was near my rooming house, was largely patronized by factory workers. Since the food was good as well as cheap, I took to eating there daily.

"The Cop" is being published for the first time in this volume.

About a week after I had become a regular patron Enzo wheeled his chair over to my table and asked abruptly, "You American or English?"

"American."

"It's plain you're not a tourist or a businessman. You eat here and not around the Via Veneto, you wear the same shoes and suit every day. You look a bit old to be a student. An artist maybe, but I don't think so. I've been scrambling my brains to guess what you're doing in Rome."

The puzzled look on his face made me laugh aloud. "Why didn't you ask me?"

He laughed also. "I like to figure things out. But now I'm asking."

"In the mornings I teach school."

"Impossible! Your Italian is as crippled as I am."

"I teach English in a private school."

Enzo struck his formidable nose with a thick finger. "Ah . . . Still and all, if the pay is low, why not go home and teach there? You'd earn more, no?"

"I want to live a year or two in Italy."

He looked amused. "At your age it must be the girls. Ours are warmer than yours, eh?"

"The girls and your pasta."

"From my pasta you'll never get sick," he said with a chuckle. "The girls you better pick with care. Penicillin is afraid of what some of our girls have."

A day later Enzo wheeled up to me and said sharply, "What's up with you, anyway? Those men who just left — you were listening so hard to their talk I could see your ears stretch. What were you writing down? If you weren't a foreigner, I'd think you were working for the police — but not experienced at it — a hell of an amateur."

I felt somewhat embarrassed, so I took the notebook out of my pocket and offered it to him. "I make notes because I'm a writer. I put down the way people talk — the expressions they use."

For a few minutes Enzo examined the notebook with intense concentration. Once he muttered, "You spell Italian worse than you speak it. You need lessons." But when he gave it back to me, his manner became cordial. "So that's why you typewrite every afternoon?"

"How do you know that?"

"One of my kitchen girls is a relative of your landlady. Well . . . so you're a writer as well as a teacher, eh? For newspapers?"

"No."

His interest in me seemed to increase. "You write books maybe?"

"So far I've only written stories."

"Ah, I see. Stories, eh? Very interesting."

Thereafter Enzo came to my table rather frequently. He asked a good many questions about life in America, but primarily he seemed interested in me because of my writing. It was puzzling because he was a man who had read little outside of newspapers and popular magazines — and yet the questions he put were of a semi-technical nature: how a writer got his ideas — what part true facts played in stories — whether it was easy or hard to write, and why. Every week there were several new questions, as though he were pondering the matter, but whenever I asked why he was so interested, he would only shrug and laugh.

When the school year ended and I told Enzo I was leaving Rome in a few days, he invited me to be his guest at a late supper. I had other plans for my remaining evenings, but he was so oddly insistent that I finally accepted. Around midnight, when we were alone in the restaurant and were starting a third bottle of wine, (Enzo having drunk two glasses to each of mine), he said rather shyly, "I have a proposition for you. You're a writer, and there's a story to my being a cripple. It's a story about . . ." he hesitated as he groped for the right words . . . "the human heart, let's say. What I mean is . . . a man has his needs, he's selfish, all men are, they're born that way. But still . . . a man pays a terrible price for thinking only about himself. It's a contradiction . . . how should a man live? . . . and why doesn't his heart tell him in the first place how to live?" He hesitated again with an embarrassed look. "This story . . . I don't mean I'm important — just another man — but maybe that's why . . . Do you understand me, maybe?"

"Yes," I said, "of course."

"Good. So my proposition is: "I'll tell you what happened to me — you put it down so people can read it. What do you say?"

"If I can, I'll be glad to."

Obviously pleased, Enzo smiled, but in a restrained way, and I could see tension instantly rising within him. He reached for the bottle of wine and re-

filled our glasses. Then he muttered, "To tell this I need
the help of the grape . . . I'll begin with . . . let's see
. . . Well, my family was of the poorest, no father, he
was killed in the First World War. When I was sixteen,
my mother got me into a seminary so I could eat and
there'd be one less hungry at home. I liked to eat, naturally, and I had love for the Madonna, but to be a
priest wasn't for me and at eighteen I left. I lived on
the edge of nothing for three years — there were millions without work — and I was so hungry sometimes
I could have eaten the devil without salt. When you're
on the bottom, my friend, your eyes see nothing good.
I decided 'all right, that's the way the world is, it's
every man for himself in a jungle.' "

Enzo drank, then moved his chair closer to mine.
"But when I was twenty-one, my luck changed — I got
the chance to be a cop. That was in the capital of a
province up north, hilly country, not many hours from
Milano. I liked being a cop — the uniform, the position it gave me, the way it made girls look at me. But
mostly I liked the chance to feather my nest. You know
how it works — the pimps, the racketeers, a businessman doing something slippery — they all pay off. The
higher you are in the police, the more you get. So I
took all I could and waited my turn to move up."

"That was in Mussolini's time, of course?"

"Yes." Mockingly Enzo gave the Fascist salute,
then spat on the floor. "A cop like I was doesn't care
who sits in the saddle. You take their pay whoever
they are, but work for yourself." He refilled his glass,
drank it off, filled it again. "Take the way I was with

women. I'm telling you exactly, no sugarcoating. A woman is to give a man pleasure, I said, and to hell with the moonshine and poetry. Let's say when I was a detective, let's say I caught some good-looking farm woman breaking a regulation, like black-marketing eggs in the war years. Did I want her to go to jail? Not especially, what for? First I'd take the basket of eggs as evidence — plenty of omelets for me there. Then I'd put my arm around her and say, 'Well, now, little chicken, you don't want to go to jail, do you?' " Most times they were too scared to do anything but curse me out a little. I didn't care about that so long as they laid down for me . . . Well, so that's the kind of man I was. I was satisfying myself and making my way in the jungle . . . But now I come to the year that did me in. It was 1943, the middle of the war, right after the Allies had taken Sicily. You remember what happened after that?"

"Not exactly," I said.

"It was complicated as hell. First, Mussolini was kicked out of the government. Then, when the Americans and British invaded down south at Salerno, the new government surrendered to them. But there were German armies in Italy. They took over by force, disarmed our army, occupied the whole country. Right away then a kind of civil war started. There were Fascists still supporting the Fritzes, and everywhere partisan groups sprang up to fight for the Allies. I admired those partisans, but I wished 'em in hell. The way I looked at it, if the Fritzes were going to be beaten, it was the Allied armies who would do it, nobody else.

What could these partisans accomplish? Nothing, it
seemed to me — kill a few soldiers, attack a supply
column — fleas biting a tiger. But what trouble they
would make for the rest of us, especially me! You see,
I knew some German from my seminary, so I'd been
assigned to the Gestapo to interpret. I liked those Gestapos the way a man likes typhus, but it seemed to me
there was only one thing to do: Wait it out, pretend I
was friendly, win their confidence. But every time those
fleas hopped the tiger snapped his tail — and I sweated.
Those Gestapos were suspicious of every Italian — and
I knew what went on in the cellar of their headquarters.
God's blood, I was scared to death they'd turn a fishy
eye on me."

Enzo drained his glass and sat for a moment in
brooding silence. His rugged face seemed to soften as
I watched him and, when he spoke, his voice had an
undertone of sadness and nostalgia. "I lived in a small
hotel on the main square. The owner had a daughter,
Grazia. I'd seen her grow up, a kid full of spirit, always running and laughing with her long hair flying.
All of a sudden she was sixteen, a woman, and I wanted
her. Any man would have. You should have seen that
girl — deep blue eyes like the sea — wheat-colored
hair down to her hips — a face so pretty and shining
your heart would melt — yet with a body so ripe a
man ached to put his hands on her. I was thirty-three,
seventeen years older, but a difference like that doesn't
mean anything if a man and a woman spark each other.
Grazia liked me well enough, and I would have been
planning day and night to be the first with her one way

or another if it hadn't been for one thing — her father. He wasn't a special friend of mine or anything like that, but it happened that he had once saved my life. For me that was the only thing on earth that made one man have a blood obligation to another. It tied me to him so that I couldn't play tricks with the girl. She had to be willing. So in my spare time I hung around when she was tending bar or doing work in the hotel. There was no mother in the way when I wanted to pay Grazia a compliment, or tease her a little . . . You know the way a man does with a virgin to pave the way. I didn't realize then how much she was in my blood, I just wanted her to start thinking about me instead of anyone else. Of course, every Fritz in town stepped into that hotel bar when he was off-duty, but with them Grazia was like ice. She was no blind little kitten about men either . . . What Italian girl is? She always wore a pin in her hair that was three inches long. 'Any man tries to force me,' she told me once, 'I'll blind him!' "

The bottle of wine was empty and Enzo wheeled behind the counter for another. He returned, opened the fresh bottle, filled his glass, and seemed not to notice that I had stopped drinking. "The trouble that came started with her father," he continued with some bitterness. "He went to Milano and didn't come back for a week. One morning I said to Grazia, 'When's your old man coming back?' She was scrubbing the floor in the lobby and she stopped and looked around — there was no one there except the desk clerk, and he was half deaf — and then she stepped up close to me with a strange look on her face.

" 'I just heard last night,' she told me, 'I've been waiting for you to come down. Poppa's not coming back.'

" 'Why not?'

" 'He sent a message. He said he expects you to watch over me while he's gone.'

" 'Where's he gone to?'

" 'He's in the hills. He's joined the Garibaldis.'

" 'Blood of the Virgin! I could break his neck!' I said.

" 'Is that how you feel about it?,' she asked me with a very disappointed look.

" 'How else? He's an imbecile. He'll get killed for nothing.'

" 'In that case you won't help?'

" 'Help who?'

" 'Poppa said you can tell me things you hear around Gestapo headquarters.'

" 'Your old man's got fried eels in his head instead of brains,' I told her. 'In the first place I don't hear anything. They don't trust me. In the second place, even if I did, what will happen if I tell you? You'll get word to him — he'll tell those other heroes — and then one day soon some of 'em will be caught and vomit out everything. Where will I be then? My feet off the ground and my neck in a noose!'

" 'Oh, I see,' she told me, 'you're a coward.'

" 'Don't use words you're too young to understand.'

" 'You've forgotten the day you were drowning and my father saved you!'

" 'Who's forgotten? Your old man wants me to watch over you. I will gladly. If you want the protection of a marriage, I'll even marry you. But I'm not having anything to do with the Garibaldis.'

"She looked at me then as though I were garbage. 'Oh,' she said very scornfully, 'I see. For my father's sake you're willing to marry me. Thanks, I'll remember. When I want to marry a bootlicker of the Gestapo, I'll whistle.' "

Enzo paused to drink a glass of wine, and then half of another. He said wryly, "It never before meant a pig's ear to me what anyone called me. A stone weighs, a word doesn't. But when Grazia called me a bootlicker of the Gestapo, I felt like whipping her behind with a wet rope. Maybe it wasn't the word, though, but the look in her eyes. It hurt my manhood to have her look at me that way. And I kept wondering about myself. Why in the name of all the Saints had I said I'd be willing to marry her? I hadn't intended to say it . . . the words just popped out. I'd never told any woman before that I'd marry her . . . it made me feel queer. Well, all the next week Grazia didn't talk to me unless she had to, as though I were a stranger or one of the Fritzes, but then something happened. The Garibaldis had been getting more active, they'd even captured an S.S. Colonel in a road ambush. The Germans put up posters offering a big reward for information about them. I said to myself, 'Aha, that's enough money to put the evil eye on them.' Then some special squads with dogs were added to the garrison in town and I said 'Aha' a second time. It was plain there was going to be a drive to clean out the hills. It happened then I got the grippe. It left me weak in the legs so I spent several days sitting in an armchair in front of my window, listening to the radio and looking out. One evening, just after dark, a man bicycled up to Gestapo headquarters on the other side of the square. It was raining hard and he had his head pulled down into his coat collar, but by the light over the doorway I spotted him right away — Gianfranco the peddler, a hunchback. He used to buy odds and ends in town — needles, thread, cooking things — and bicycle into the hills to sell to the farmers and sheep-herders. I knew him well because years ago I'd fooled around with a niece of his. When I saw the guards take him inside, I remembered something: He always was a Mussolini lover, used to strut with the blackshirts in every parade. So I thought to myself, 'Money doesn't stink, eh, Gianfranco?' After twenty minutes he came out, looked around carefully, then bicycled over to the hotel. Soon as he went inside I forgot my weak legs and went downstairs. Like I expected, he was at the bar. The place was full of Germans so I watched from outside. Gianfranco had three quick drinks in a row. When he was paying his bill, I went out to the lobby. I waited until he was outside and then took a look. He was bicycling in the direction of the hills. So then I sat down to think it over. It was perfectly clear what was up. The only question in my mind was should I tip off Grazia? I knew it would sweeten her toward me a lot if I did — but I wanted to be sure there was no way it could make trouble for me. It seemed to me there wasn't any, so I decided. Grazia was serving some soldiers at the bar. I couldn't be sure one of 'em didn't understand Italian so I tapped her on the shoulder and said, 'There's a phone call from Milano, I think it's your old man.' I walked back to the lobby and a minute later she came running out. I said, 'There's no phone call, but something's up. We have to talk private.' Grazia was suspicious, but she led me down the hall to her room. When I closed the door, she said, 'Don't try locking it.'

" 'And don't you be such a scared virgin. What do you take me for?' I told her, almost yelling. It burned me to have her speak like that. 'What was that pig-faced Gianfranco drinking?'

" 'Grappa. Why?'

" 'Has he been in your bar before this?'

" 'What are you trying to do,' she asked very coldly, 'make a police spy out of me?'

" 'I'm remembering your old man saved my life. Maybe now I'll do the same for him, the imbecile. Answer my question.'

"She looked at me with big eyes then, suddenly scared. 'Gianfranco's come in now and then, not often.'

" 'Those other times — did he drink grappa?'

"She thought for a second. 'No, ordinary wine, never more than one small glass.'

" 'So for him he spent big tonight, hey?'

" 'Yes.'

" 'When he paid you, did you see how much money he had?'

" 'No.' She put her hand on my arm. 'Enzo, what's this got to do with my father?'

" 'Nobody knows the hills better than that son of

a whore, Gianfranco. Just before he bought himself that grappa he was in Gestapo headquarters.'

"Grazia said, *'Madonna mia,'* and started to tremble. 'So what do you think?'

" 'I think he got a first payment on the reward. If I'm right, I don't believe the Germans will lose time. I think they'll move troops during the night and attack as soon as it's light enough to see.'

" *'Jesu é mari,'* Grazia said, 'may I be split in four parts if I don't put a knife in his dirty heart one day.'

" 'Never mind that now,' I told her. 'Have you got any way to send a warning?'

" 'Yes,' she told me. She was white as paper.

" 'In time for them to get away?'

" 'I hope so.'

" 'Now look,' I told her, *'leave me out of it!* Nobody has to know who tipped you off.'

" 'Sure, Enzo,' she said, 'of course.'

"As I was opening the door, she kissed me on the cheek. I didn't realize then what the kiss meant to me. All I thought was, 'Fine, I've sweetened her up, I'll be quits with her old man, there'll be nothing in the way.' I went back to my room and sat down in the dark to watch the square. The rain had stopped, there was nothing stirring. Ten minutes later there was a knock on the door. It was Grazia and she was shaking. She said, 'I can't send anyone. I called the only two contacts I have. They're not home.' And then she gave me one in the belly. *'I'm* going. I know where they are. Will you give me a gun, Enzo?'

"In that moment I saw the handwriting on the

wall. Grazia would be captured and the Gestapo would learn the part I'd played in her going. But how could I stop her? I wasn't thinking of her, you see, only of myself.

" 'Will you give me a gun?' she asked me a second time.

" 'Don't talk nonsense,' I yelled at her. 'I only have one gun and the number's registered. You wouldn't know how to use it anway.'

" 'But just listen why,' she begged me. 'The Germans might get there before me, but if it's still dark, I can shoot in the air as a warning.'

" 'I can't give it to you!'

"She started out, but I caught her arm. I said, 'Grazia, maybe I can help. How far do you have to go?'

"For a second she stared at me in a way I can see yet . . . a look of hope in her eyes you couldn't put into words. I saw what she was thinking . . . that *I* would go. 'It's about twenty kilometers by road,' she told me. 'But who knows how roundabout I'll have to go to avoid patrols?' She kept looking at me with her heart in her eyes, but I closed my mind to her the way you shut a door. I was too afraid to go and I cursed the Garibaldis, and I only wanted to find a way to stop her from going.

" 'It's crazy,' I told her. 'It's already eight o'clock. To get there in time you've got to arrive by four in the morning at the latest. How can you cover twenty-five or thirty kilometers on foot in eight hours — when it's dark, when you'll have to cross fields, climb over fences, maybe hide?'

" 'I'll run part of the time.'

" 'Without using a flashlight?'

" 'I'll use a small one when I have to. I've got to try, don't I? Is there any other way?' She waited for a moment and then, when I didn't say anything, she pulled her arm loose and started for the door. I felt so sick and scared that all I could do was yell at her, 'So at least put on a black dress, you little fool. Take a piece of charcoal to rub on your face if you get in a spot. Take a club against dogs. And some food to keep up your strength — sugar, cheese, bread, especially sugar.'

"She didn't say anything. She just looked at me with a stony face and left."

For a moment Enzo interrupted his narrative. He peered intensely at me with eyes that had become bloodshot. He was leaning forward, his hands gripping the arms of his chair. "I let her go like that, a sixteen-year-old girl. My mind wasn't on her, I was scared only for me. The minute she was gone I sat down and tried to make a plan for myself. The only really safe thing was to run. With my credentials I didn't have to worry about curfew, I could move at night. Who could give me a safe hideout? From my police experience I knew that to stay in hiding for months took very favorable conditions — the right place, friends willing to risk their own necks, even the right neighbors often. I couldn't think of anyone. To keep moving from one city to the next was no good either — there was too much danger of being nabbed in a bus or railroad station where they were always checking papers. Some-

thing occurred to me after awhile that seemed first-
rate. The Swiss border was only sixty kilometers away.
On a bicycle I could be there in good time. I'd go direct
to the border guards with my credentials and my interpreter's card. I'd tell 'em I was after an underground
leader who was expected to cross. I felt absolutely con-
fident that after a bit of talk I'd know where their
guards were stationed — and where I could cross safe.
I'd be in Switzerland before daylight."

Enzo laughed softly, ironically, and, in a curious
gesture, slapped one of his stumps several times with
the back of his hand. "So," he said, "I had a plan, I
felt safe enough to breathe easy — and right then I
began to think of Grazia. I imagined her running
through the night, that little kid. I gave her one chance
in a hundred of not being caught. And then, like somebody had hit me on the skull with a hammer, I began
to think what would happen to her in the cellar of the
Gestapo. I broke out in a sweat, I got so sick to my
stomach that I almost vomited. I told myself again
and again that I ought to start moving, but my legs
stayed where they were. I could see Grazia's eyes as
she'd looked at me, waiting with so much hope for me
to say I'd go in her place. She knew that as a cop I
could have gone by bicycle. It would have been risky,
but a hundred times less than for her. Why had I shut
my mind to it? I began to curse myself. I looked into
the mirror and spat and told myself I deserved to live
blind and hungry for ninety-nine years. For the first
time in my life, y'see, there was someone who meant
more to me than my own skin. I wanted Grazia to be
safe — God, how I wanted it. It wasn't that I wanted

her for myself, I just wanted *her* to be safe. So, even though I told myself again and again that I ought to start moving, I sat all night long like a paralytic. Like I'd expected, at four in the morning the Germans were on the move in the direction of the hills — motorcycles, armored cars, trucks with infantry. At six-thirty a staff car came back and drove into the closed yard alongside Gestapo headquarters. I could see only the driver. Then, at seven-fifteen, *I* got a call — whether I was sick or not, they wanted me at headquarters right away."

Enzo's bloodshot eyes were staring at the empty darkness of the restaurant. He had stopped drinking. His hands were gripped together, the fingers were working. "I was sick all right," he muttered, "but not from the grippe. Did they have Grazia or didn't they? As I crossed the square, I felt as though I wouldn't make it to the other side. My knees were weak, I had such pain in my temples I almost couldn't keep from groaning out loud."

For a few moments Enzo fell silent, but then he shook himself out of his reverie. He said painfully, "I was sent in to the Commissar, Brandt. He'd been a cop like me before he got into the Gestapo, but high up, chief of detectives in some city, a man about sixty. He was sharper than I was and I knew it, one of those who never show what they're thinking or feeling, with a face like granite. I hated him, and I was afraid of him. First he asked me how I was feeling, not that he cared a damn, and I said I was a little shaky in the legs. Then he asked, 'Did you hear the troop movement this morning?'

" 'Yes, Herr Commissar,' I answered. 'It woke me up.'

" 'That was a raiding party,' he told me. 'We had information about a partisan hideout — a cave in the hills.' He stopped talking then, keeping his eyes on me, and I almost jumped out of my skin. I was so scared I got a strange, crazy thought — I wished I had a bag of salt so that I could sprinkle the floor with it for good luck the way some peasants do in a new house. It was completely crazy. Anyway, Brandt went on talking. He said, 'The approach to the cave was kept under observation last night by three men friendly to us . . . '

" 'Gianfranco and his two brothers,' I thought to myself.

" 'These men,' the Commissar said, 'were stationed thirty meters apart along the bank of a small stream. The cave was about two-hundred meters on the other side. Our troops were to reach the area at five o'clock. Twenty minutes before they arrived the partisans were given a warning and got away.' "

Almost whispering Enzo said to me, "When I heard that, I thought I'd explode with excitement at what little Grazia had done. But a second later I felt like Brandt had shoved a towel down my gullet and I was strangling. 'The warning came from a girl,' he told me, 'the bar girl in your hotel.'

"I pretended surprise as best I could. 'Grazia? I never would have guessed her out of the whole town.'

" 'Why?'

" 'She's a kid. How did she get involved?'

" 'Yes, how?' Brandt asked sarcastically. 'Just a

pretty, innocent, little girl, good Catholic, too, I'm sure. She was jumped by one of the men when she got near the stream — and she put a bread knife into his chest so hard she couldn't get it out. When the others came at her, she ran into the stream — screaming to the partisans that German soldiers were coming. She screamed quite a number of times before they shut her up . . . Well, Enzo?'

" 'Well what? Herr Commissar,' I asked.

" 'What do you conclude from this?'

"I took off my raincoat to gain a moment's time. Then I said, 'Seems like the partisans have a group in town . . . and a good intelligence service.'

" 'Agreed.'

" 'But isn't it strange,' I went on, 'that they'd send a girl on a mission like that?'

" 'She got there,' Brandt said, 'so maybe they knew what they were doing. Anyway, she's our key. I've already questioned her, but she's being very patriotic. As you know, my Italian is not so good. I'm not sure she understood me entirely. Right now she's getting some special attention. When she comes back, you talk to her. I want her to know what her situation is without any mistake. If she'll give us the names of everyone in the group, she can go back to tending bar. If she doesn't, I won't leave her alone until she's in little pieces.' "

Sixteen years had passed since Brandt had said this to Enzo, but as he repeated it to me now his tone became a whimper. " 'Until she's in little pieces,' " he said a second time. "You can't know what those words did to me . . . how frightful I felt, how guilty. I *had*

to ask what was being done to her. It was a risky question, I was not supposed to know what went on in the
cellar, or ask what 'special attention' meant. My tongue
felt big as a sausage, I could hardly wag it. I said,
'Herr Commissar . . . I know this girl well and I have
an idea how to handle her . . . but first . . . if I may
ask . . . it will affect what I say . . . what's she getting
. . . the attention I mean?'

"Brandt gave me a long, cold look. 'What's the
matter with you?' he asked. 'You're sweating, your
voice is trembling . . .'

" 'I'm still not over the grippe,' I answered as
easily as I could. 'It's not important.'

"He looked at me a moment longer, then he said,
'I'd like the girl to work for us from now on so I
thought I'd try giving her a shock as a first step —
nothing that would stop her from being in the hotel
as usual tomorrow. I told the boys to line up and have
some fun with her.' "

A twisted, sad little smile came to Enzo's lips as
he told me this. Gazing at me, he said softly, "Now, pay
attention to what can happen to the human heart. For
a few moments I thought I'd go out of control. But
why? I already knew she was being tortured. Was it
any worse for poor Grazia to be raped by half a dozen
men than to be beaten with clubs, or have her nails
pulled out? Perhaps not as bad. You might say because
I loved her I was made wild by just thinking of it. No,
it was something worse. It was like I was having a
nightmare where many things were happening at the
same time. I felt as though I was inside Grazia's flesh,

inside her heart, that I was weeping her tears and feeling her shame — and yet at the same time *I saw myself as one of the men who were raping her.* Hadn't I taken women who didn't want me — not by direct force, maybe — but by other ways that amounted to the same? And if not for Grazia's father, I would have played any trick to have her. Right then I saw the man I was — no different from those pigs in the cellar! Ah, Mother of God, it's impossible for me to explain to you, to put into words what happened inside of me then — like a volcano vomiting everything out of its belly. But I remember every thought, every feeling. And I remember saying to myself, 'All right, you coward, you stinking swine with sewage in your veins, you have one thing, a gun. When they bring in Grazia, you'll shoot Brandt, and then her, and then yourself.' "

Again the twisted, sad little smile came to Enzo's lips. "As you see," he said, "I didn't shoot myself, or them either. After a while two S.S. men brought Grazia into the office. She was walking, but like in a stupor, and she was crying . . . my God . . . that crying, not loud, but every part of her body crying to Heaven. They put her down in a chair and she fell off it and lay like a rag doll that a child throws away."

Enzo paused. He was weeping now, silently, the tears running down his craggy cheeks. "She was wearing a black skirt and sweater . . . I remember some buttons on the side of the skirt were missing. Her legs were bare . . . and streaked with blood. Brandt saw the blood and smiled like with surprise. He said to the S.S. men, 'Don't tell me an Italian girl her age could still be a virgin?' Both of the men laughed and one said, 'We were surprised, too.' Brandt waved them out. To me he said, 'She'll talk now, I think. Go ahead with her . . . ' It was then I changed my mind about what to do. I said, 'Yes, Herr Commissar,' and walked over to Grazia. I raised her up and sat her against the wall. I said, 'Grazia, this is Enzo,' over and over again. Her crying started to die down and her eyes began to see me. I asked Brandt for some water. When he brought it, I put the glass to her lips and ordered her to drink. She took a little, then suddenly drank it all down like she was parched. I said, 'Grazia, look at me. Do you know me?' She looked and gave a little nod. I said, 'Watch me!' I took my revolver out. 'Do you see this?' She nodded again. 'Watch carefully now,' I said — and I snapped up and pointed the gun at Brandt."

There was a moment's pause while Enzo's fingers worked in his lap. "You'll see," he told me, sadly and bitterly, "I did everything right . . . I thought every next step out fine — except for one thing. I said to Brandt, 'I'm so close to shooting that if you make one little move I don't order, you're finished. Get over there.' I put him to one side of the door so that if it opened, he wouldn't be seen — facing the wall with his hands on it. When I frisked him, I found a knife in a belt sheath as well as his Luger. Then I backed off so I could see Grazia while I watched him and the door. She was sitting up stiff now. I said 'Listen Grazia, I'm taking you out of here. Do you understand me? Answer!'

" 'Yes, Enzo,' she said. It took effort for her to speak. 'I understand, Enzo.'

" 'Can you walk? Stand up.'

"She got herself up, but then had to catch hold of the back of the chair. " 'Are you dizzy?' I asked.

" 'A little,' she said. 'But I'll be able to walk, Enzo. Oh, Enzo, *please* take me out of here. If you can't, then shoot me, *please*. Promise to shoot me, Enzo. Swear by the Virgin.'

" 'Yes, I promise,' I told her, 'but be quiet now.' It was almost more than I could bear to have her saying, 'Enzo, Enzo,' as though I was her savior instead of the coward who had gotten her into this. I went for my raincoat and hung it over my arm so it would hide the pistol. Then I went over to Brandt. I said to him, 'Listen with care: As one cop to another, you want to live and I've got no reason to do you in. I'm no partisan, but I want this girl. If you act sensible, you'll be free in half an hour. You want to strike a bargain on that?'

" 'Sure,' he said. 'What do you want me to do?'

"I told him then — he was to stay three steps in front of me and the girl. We'd go straight to the courtyard and get into a car. He'd drive. Once we were in the hills, I'd let him out. But if he tried anything at all, I'd plug him.

" 'Don't worry,' he said. 'I'm no fool.'

"And that's how it went," Enzo said. "I put my left arm around Grazia and kept my gun arm free. From the office to the courtyard was not far — down one stairway, through a door. We passed only one S.S. man and the guard in the lobby. There was a platoon of men in the yard, but Brandt hollered for a car and there were no questions. I put Grazia in the back and said for her to lie down. I got in with Brandt and told him to start easy until we were a block away and then go fast. In fifteen minutes we were outside the town, and twenty minutes after that we were high in the hills and I told him to stop. I was feeling so good, so damn excited, that I couldn't help making a game of it. I said, 'Tell me the truth. You think I'll plug you now?'

" 'We had a bargain,' he answered. 'Like you said, we're both cops. I'm sure you won't.'

" 'That's right,' I told him, 'but maybe Grazia feels different. You want to shoot him, Grazia?'

"She answered . . . I tell you she answered like a bride at the altar saying yes . . . I took the Luger out of my pocket, cocked it, and held it out to her."

Enzo gazed at me and smiled bitterly. "So there we were — in a German staff car parked in the hills — a neat little target for any partisans who were around — the one thing I hadn't given mind to. So a tommy-gun hit us from one side, and grenades from another. When I came to, I was in the partisan camp and everybody was sorry, but how did they know who was in the car? I had no legs . . . Brandt was dead . . . and my little Grazia was dead, too."

Enzo turned away from me and stared at the empty darkness of the cafe. He said slowly, "So there you are, my friend, that's my story. It seems to me . . . how much I've thought about it! . . . that . . . well, take insects now . . . whatever it is insects have, instinct they say . . . they know how to live their lives. But we who are human beings . . . we have such awful mixed up hearts . . . and what things they make us do, eh?"